YOURS TO CONQUER

A PURE DECADENCE NOVEL

KELLY COLLINS

BOOK NOOK PRESS

Copyright © 2015 by Kelly Collins

No part of this publication may be reproduced, distributed, or transmitted in any form or by any means, including photocopying, recording, or other electronic or mechanical methods, without the prior written permission of the publisher, except as permitted by U.S. copyright law. For permission requests, contact kelly@authorkellycollins.com.

The story, all names, characters, and incidents portrayed in this production are fictitious. No identification with actual persons (living or deceased), places, buildings, and products is intended or should be inferred. All products or brand names are trademarks of their respective owners.

A big thanks to my husband, whose patience and love are never ending. You rescued me decades ago and you're still my hero. To Nik, Alec, and Gabby for keeping me on toes and making every day worth living.

CHAPTER ONE

I've been selling my time for years now. Rates start at one hundred dollars an hour, with a three-hour minimum. I'm not selling my body; at least not in the way most people think. If I were selling sex, I would charge a hell of a lot more. You don't get acquainted with my girlie parts for money. I will gift you with my body if I think you're worthy, but never as a client.

I didn't grow up thinking, *I'll be an escort*—it just happened. One day while I was at Java Joes, a nice-looking businessman asked me if I'd be willing to accompany him to his Christmas party. He was kind, and I had no plans. I told him to take a seat, and we would talk over the details. What he wanted was a pretty young girl to rub in the face of his ex-wife. She married his co-worker, who was also attending the party. We brokered a deal right then. He'd buy me a pretty cocktail dress, and I'd hang on his every word for the evening. There would be no sex; it was strictly a business arrangement. That's how this escort thing got started. We attended a Christmas party and made quite a splash. I became a regular on Dillon's arm for months. He never expected anything from me except my company. He helped me come up with my original business model and introduced me to most of my clientele. He spread the word, and before I knew it, I had a group of regulars who kept me busy nearly every night of the week.

I learned a lot from the experience. One of the most profound lessons was that most men are decent. I also learned the majority of them are not looking for happily ever after. The men I meet don't have time to build relationships. They're more interested in conquering the world than winning a woman's fickle heart. They buy what they want, and they're not cheap when it comes to quality. *I'm* quality.

There's a market for girls like me. Attractive and intelligent women who will dress up, look pretty, and smile. I work out, eat right, and take care of myself. I can hold a conversation with just about anyone. I stay on top of current affairs and research my clients and their businesses.

Most of my time is spent bridging gaps for people. I'm a social ambassador, if you will. I make people feel at ease in awkward situations. It's pretty boring, but every once in a while you meet someone special.

Four months ago, I met Anthony, and he changed my life.

EVEN IN HIS SLEEP, he keeps me close. He hangs his arm across my body and pulls me tightly against him. With my head against his chest, I listen to the beat of his heart and the slow, steady rhythm of his breathing. I inhale the scent of him and realize I'm happy to stay like this all day.

Lying here, I reflect on our first date. It seems like a lifetime ago, but it's been just a few months. He took me to his restaurant, where he wined and dined me as if I were royalty. He picked out a special menu and fed me himself. I remember licking butter sauce from his fingers. Every bite was a sensual experience. He teased me all night, making sexual innuendos about everything. He drove me crazy as I watched his tongue slide in and out of his mouth. I nearly came undone when he informed me he had an oral fixation and he planned on tasting every inch of my body. There was so much electricity in the air, we could have powered the city. I knew immediately I wouldn't be sleeping alone that night.

We spent our first night at his Malibu home. Perched above the ocean, his house sat like a sentinel, guarding his private little beach. It was like a fairy tale, and he was my Prince Charming, my knight in shining armor, and the house was his castle.

I felt like the only girl in the world until I opened his bathroom drawer and found dozens of toothbrushes for his "guests." I teased him about having so many, but he didn't blink an eye. One thing about Anthony, is that he makes no excuses for himself. In that way, we are very much alike.

I feel him stretch, his hands reaching far above his head. His chest puffs out as he takes a big cleansing breath and exhales with a groan. "Morning, Red. How did you sleep, baby?" He pulls me on top of his chest and holds me tightly. The coarse hairs tickle my cheek. "That was a fabulous party last night. It's so good to see Damon get his shit straight," he says. A final groan escapes as his stretch ends.

Kat and Damon are our friends. I introduced them on the same day I met Anthony. They hit it off, but for whatever reason, Damon's demons nearly got the best of them. Last night's party was Damon's way of letting Kat know she's the only one for him. He carried her out of the party, and I imagine we won't hear from them for a while.

"I'm glad those two figured it out. It was so hard to watch them self-destruct when we both knew they needed each other so badly. I thought the way he gave her a letter from his dentist was adorable." Kat had indicated to Damon that she had two prerequisites for dating. One was that he had to have nice teeth, and the second was that he couldn't be a serial killer.

3

"I remember a girl who required a note from my doctor saying I was disease-free before she'd have sex without a condom. The irony is that she was an escort, and I was merely a chef. You would've thought it should be the other way around."

I laugh. "I remember a man who raced to the doctor when he knew he would get a blow job if he could produce a clean bill of health. The girl in question was an escort, not a hooker, and she gave up her job when she started hanging out with the chef."

"The chef didn't ask her to give up her job, but it relieved him when she did. He was concerned he would have to use his knife skills on something other than vegetables. He would've killed anyone who touched her."

"I love my chef, his knife skills, and his other skills," I tease as I place a kiss on his chest.

"Oh, you like my skills, huh? Let me show you some skills, babe," he growls as he rolls on top of me, pressing me into the mattress. I love the feel of his body on me, the weight of him as he pins me down. I never tire of what we do for each other. I inhale sharply as he slides inside of me. His body fills mine completely, and my heart skips a beat every time we make love. I wonder if that feeling will ever go away. I guess if it does, then it's time to move on.

Anthony takes me slowly. He has never been one to rush; it's all about the details to him. Once his creative juices get flowing, he ignites me. His slow pace always gives me time to build up to the most glorious release. I love mornings like this—mornings where we have nowhere to be and nothing to do. This is what life is all about—connection.

I curl into his body and listen to his breath even out. My hand trails up the hairline to his belly button. The rumble of his stomach makes me giggle. Now that he's fed his first hunger, he needs to address his appetite for food.

"What do you want for breakfast, babe? I can make your favorite pancakes, or I can make you a bacon and veggie omelet. What will it be?"

"You know you'll get brownie points for either, so you decide." It's sweet that he gives me a choice. In the end, he'll make what he wants, anyway.

"I'm counting on the brownie points; I've been collecting them for months. I figure someday I'm going to screw something up, and I'll need to cash in." He rolls out of bed, throws on his shorts, and runs upstairs to start breakfast.

I slowly get up and make my way to the bathroom. The girl in the mirror looks happy. I tell her that she's the luckiest woman in the world. So much about that statement rings true, and yet so much of it's a lie. Pulling myself together, I throw on my robe and head upstairs.

As I near the top step, I inhale the unmistakable scent of bacon. Who doesn't love bacon? I think it should be in its own food group, right at the top of the food pyramid. I follow the aroma to the kitchen where a shirtless Anthony cracks eggs with one hand and whisks them with the other. I slide onto the center stool at the island and watch him create the perfect omelet with ease. He moves around the kitchen effortlessly. He's definitely in his element. Watching him is like watching a conductor lead the orchestra. He has the art of cooking finely tuned and perfectly harmonized. Pouring freshly brewed coffee into two mugs, he places a steaming hot cup in front of me.

"Do you ever tire of cooking?" I ask as I take a sip. He makes the best coffee, even better than what Kat brought me from Java Joes when she used to work there.

"I love cooking for you, Em. I don't get to be in the kitchen in my own restaurants very much anymore. I made you a bacon and garden veggie omelet. Enjoy." He places two plates on the breakfast bar and comes around to sit beside me. "I love the look on your face when you taste something that you like. Your eyes roll back into your head, and it's erotic to watch."

I take my first bite, savor the taste, then exhale. "I love that you cook for me. You know I love food. In fact, I love most foods, except for lima beans, lentils, and brussels sprouts. You'll never elicit that response from those foods." The thought of lima beans makes me scrunch up my nose in distaste.

"I don't like lima beans either, so you'll never find them on my menu. They're too chalky tasting for me. Lentils, if cooked properly, can be quite nice. Brussels sprouts, on the other hand, are fabulous. You don't like them because no one has made them like I do. Someday I'll make you brussels sprouts, and your body will shudder with delight."

"Until that day, I reserve the right to dislike them," I say as I gobble up the omelet. "This is amazing," I sigh and give him the satisfied look he craves. "What makes it so good? It's just veggies, bacon, and eggs."

"I make it good. Without me, it's just an omelet." There's that cocky arrogance that I love. Anthony has a swagger to him that most men can't pull off, but on him—it's sexy. He takes my empty plate and walks over to the sink.

"Since you cooked, I'll clean." I stand beside him and bump him out of the way with my hip. He steps aside and watches me while I wash up. He is *always* watching me. He moves behind me and threads his hands under my arms, rubbing my stomach.

"I love having you here. I thought I was going to get you out of my system that first night. When that didn't work, I took you to Catalina so I could spend the week trying to erase you from my mind. That didn't work either. It's been nearly four months, and I still want you as much as I did then."

CHAPTER TWO

I lean my head against his chest as he kisses my neck. His hands tug at the tie that holds my robe together. As it falls open, I can feel the cool morning air against my skin. Anthony's hands run up my stomach and settle on my breasts. He caresses my skin as a soft moan escapes my mouth.

I love his hands. I've spent many hours looking at them and have them memorized. His right index finger has a small scar across the middle knuckle. It happened before he mastered his knife skills in culinary school. His hands are soft with nicely groomed nails. It surprises me how such large hands can be so tender and loving. I've watched what hands can do when they're angry, but Anthony has only used his hands to create beauty and passion.

"Hey, babe, where did you go? I lost you there for a minute. What are you thinking about?" He turns me in his arms to look into my eyes.

"I was thinking about your hands and how you always use them for pleasure, never for pain."

"I would never lay a hand on you unless I meant it to give you pleasure. I know your life had been tough. You have some awful memories, but those are in the past, and no one will ever lay a hand on you again." He pulls me into his arms and holds me tightly.

"Did you know my mom died twelve years ago this week?" I ask with a sigh.

"I didn't know. It would help if you shared these things with me. We can get through the tough times together." His big blue eyes are full of concern.

"I was standing here with your hands on me, wondering if she ever felt like this in her life. Did she ever get to feel the soft caress of a man's hand on her body? Or was it always the sharp sting of an angry slap?"

"I don't know, but I can promise you I'll never hurt you with these hands." He raises them, slightly wiggling his fingers before lowering them back down and around my waist. "I want to use my hands to make you scream in passion, never in pain." He lowers his head and presses his lips to mine. My arms encircle his neck as my legs wrap around his waist. Cupping my bottom, he carries me with ease onto the deck and lowers us onto the chaise lounge. Turning me effortlessly in his arms, he settles me between his legs and wraps around me in a protective embrace. I look out over the ocean as the waves lap gently onto the shore.

"We've never talked about it, but I want to know what happened when you were a kid, Em. I know your dad was abusive; you've alluded to that. I need to know what you went through so I can help when things get you down. You're a woman who loves passionately, and yet I always feel you're holding something back. It's like you're afraid of losing yourself, so you refuse to let your guard down." Pulling me deeper against his chest, he continues. "I haven't pried because our relationship was new, and we were busy with the grand opening of *Ahz*. Now that things are slowing down, I want to take more time to get to know you. I know you physically, like the back of my hand, but I want to know what's going on in your pretty little head. I want to earn your trust, Em. You need to be able to depend on me."

I curl up onto his lap as he holds me against him, and I breathe deeply before I tell him my truth.

"My dad is a long-haul truck driver. He was gone most of the time. I always wondered why he would choose to be away from his family when he could've worked locally. Sometimes he'd be gone for weeks. Those were wonderful weeks. My mom was relaxed and carefree. She smiled a lot when he was gone." I take a breath, deciding where I want to go with my story. Do I give him the rose-colored version, or do I give him the hard, gritty truth?

"We'd cuddle up on the couch together and watch movies like *Sixteen Candles* and *The Breakfast Club*. I'd see her eyes tear up during the romantic parts, and I often wondered what was behind those tears. Being twelve, I had no idea what happened in a grownup's life.

"She was my protector, and for as long as I can remember, she defended me. He was always mad at me. I did nothing to deserve his wrath, but somehow I was always his target. I could sit at the table coloring, and he would lash out at me. If I were in the way, he would push me or knock me down. My mom would always rush in to intervene. She often stepped between us, forcing him to take his anger out on her.

"When he came home, he always smelled of cigarettes and alcohol. She would shuffle me off to my room or send me to Kat's for the night. I'd hide in my locked room and listen to her screaming and crying. She was always bruised and bleeding when he left." I pause as I remember the last day I saw her. She was beautiful with her long brown hair pulled back in a barrette and her green eyes brighter and happier than I've ever seen. I left for school without a care in the world.

"I don't understand, Em. You told me that your dad was gone, and by the way you're talking, it sounds as if he's still alive and kicking. Can you clarify, babe? I want to understand." His voice is soft and calm as he pulls me out of my deep thoughts. He has a soothing effect on my raw nerves. I hate talking about my past; it brings back such painful memories. I've seen horrifying things happen. I watched my mom get her heart ripped out and her ass beat over and over. I'm afraid of giving my heart away. The little bit I keep for myself protects me from being completely vulnerable.

"I told you he was gone, but I never said he was dead. He is gone, has been for a long time. I haven't seen him since the funeral. The only time he has contacted me over the years has been to throw accusations and spew venom in my direction."

"I misunderstood. I'm sorry," he says as he places a gentle kiss on the top of my head. "Go on."

I pause for a minute as I look out at the ocean. The water is almost glass-like, except for the gentle waves that are breaking on the shore. The view is a stark contrast to the storm I feel inside of my body.

"I don't know what happened that last day. I came home from school, and he was there. I snuck in the front door and hid in the living room. He was yelling at her. He told her he was working hard to support her and her kid, and the least she could do was lay on her back when he got home. He said, 'her kid' like I didn't belong to him. The tone in his voice terrified me. I ran straight to my bedroom as soon as I heard him yelling. There was so much noise." I pull my hands to my ears, covering them as if it will help silence the memory. "I can hear breaking glass like it was yesterday. She must have heard me come in because she screamed for me to go to Kat's." Tears slip from my eyes while I tell the story. "I was afraid to walk out the front door, so I climbed out of my bedroom window like a coward. I heard the unmistakable sound of him hitting her. There is a sound that a fist makes when it crushes bone, and that's the sound I heard as I jumped from my window ledge to the ground. She screamed that she hated him. I ran to Kat's."

"Did you always go to Kat's when things got bad?" His large palm strokes my hair softly, and his voice coaxes me to continue.

"Yes, they always took me in. I'm pretty sure they knew what my life was like. It would be hard not to notice that every time my dad came home, my mom had horrific accidents. There was a range of injuries, from burns to broken bones, but his favorite was punching and kicking my mom in the stomach. No one but me got to see those injuries. I only saw them because I would have to help her bind herself to stabilize her broken ribs."

"How did your mom die?" His voice is quiet. I can sense he's afraid to ask the question. I'm not sure I want to answer it. It is hands down the most painful day of my life.

"I want to say he killed her. Deep down inside, I know that it's true. He didn't deliver the final blow, but he did enough that night to make her run. At some point, she packed up the car. I know she was planning to take me away because my clothes were there as well. Video footage shows her filling the car up with gas at the Shell on Baldwin Avenue. The video is grainy, but you can see she was beaten badly. Her left eye was swollen shut, and her right eye was not much better. She pulled out of the parking lot, and she must not have seen the semi coming. They said she died instantly." Tears are spilling from my eyes at the memory.

"Oh, God, babe, I had no idea. I'm so sorry. I thought it was just an accident." He pulls me close. "I got you. It's going to be okay," he whispers in my ear. I bury my face in his bare chest and cry. It's been a long time since I've cried. In fact, I don't think I ever really had time to grieve the loss of my mom. It forced me into self-preservation mode the minute she died.

"It was an accident," I say as I wipe the tears from my eyes. "We buried what was left of her three days later, and my dad took off on his next run. My aunt came to stay with me during the week. I stayed at Kat's on the weekend. Eventually, I ended up spending more time at Kat's house than my own. The mortgage got paid until my eighteenth birthday, and then he sold the house. I was on my own from that point on. I got a note from him four years ago, saying something about me being a whore like my mother. My best guess was he found out that I was an escort and just assumed I was selling it all." I feel as if I've bared my soul to Anthony. I curl up in his lap, trying to protect what is left of me.

"If he ever comes around you again, I want to know. I don't care if it's a note, a call, or a visit. You belong to me, and I take care of what's mine."

"I belong to you? Since when do I belong to you?" This bit of information is surprising to me. How did we get from *I'm a confirmed bachelor* to *you're mine* in less than four months?

"Since the day I threw all the extra toothbrushes away," he says as he tickles me. The way he runs his fingers up my sides makes me laugh uncontrollably. "There's the girl I love. The one with the robust laugh."

There are tears in my eyes again, but this time they are caused by joy and playfulness. He has tickled the sadness out of me.

CHAPTER THREE

The sun feels fabulous against my skin. Anthony's private little beach is the perfect place to work on your tan. His house sits in a little alcove. There are rocky outcroppings on both sides, providing privacy in such a way that you can't see the neighbors on either side. It's almost like having your own little island. As I look out to the ocean, I find it peaceful, not a ship or sailboat in sight.

"I brought you some iced tea and the sunscreen." Anthony plops down beside me, kicking up sand as he settles into his spot. "Let me slather you up. I don't want you getting burned." I hum with pleasure as he rubs sunscreen on my body.

"How did I get so lucky to have you? You cook, you clean, and you're a stud in the sack," I tease, but as I look at him, I can see that his expression is serious. "What's up? You look like you're frowning." I watch him as he seems to struggle internally with something. My heart pounds wildly. Did I scare him away with the truth of my childhood?

"I've been thinking about something since we spoke earlier today. It was something that you said when we were talking about your parents." I bring myself to a sitting position so the sun's glare doesn't disrupt my view. My heart drops into my stomach.

"What did I say?" I ask and wonder what I could have said to him that would cause him to ponder it since this morning.

"You said that he talked to your mom like you weren't his kid. That he was always gone, and you wondered why a father would want to be away from his family. The thing that bothered me the most was when you described the note he sent to you four years ago. Would you mind if I hired someone to look into your mom's past?"

"My mom wasn't a whore, Anthony. If you think you'll find out that she was, then you're wrong." I am furious he thinks my mom had a sordid past. I try to twist away from him, so he doesn't see the anger in my eyes.

His hands come to my shoulders, and he forces me to face him. "I don't think your mother was a whore, babe. I think your dad isn't your dad, and I wonder if I can find out the reason you ended up with him as your father." He pulls me into his arms. "I love you, and I want to figure out a way to help you understand your past. I know it weighs heavily on your mind." His hands tenderly rub my back. My heartbeat normalizes.

"I'm sorry. I didn't mean to get angry with you. It's just that my dad was always saying mean things about my mom, and I feel like I need to protect her...or at least my memory of her." I lean into his embrace, knowing I'm safe in his arms.

"I understand. I'd do the same if anyone said a bad thing about my mom. You already know that I think my mom is a saint."

I lean back and look into his eyes. "Your mom is a saint; she raised you, and that couldn't have been easy," I tease, feeling better than I did a few minutes ago.

"I want to do this, Em. I have a gut feeling about something. Do I have your permission?" I stare into his eyes and see the pleading look. He loves me, and I love him. I can't deny him anything.

"I don't want you to waste your money. I think my mom would have told me if I wasn't his kid."

"So, is that a no? Or is it a, 'you can do what you want, and I won't stop you, even though I think you'll find nothing?'" His head tilts to the side in question.

"You can do what you want. However, I don't think you'll find anything." Trying to lighten the mood, I add, "I've had a passing hope that somehow I was switched at birth or something crazy like that. I am the only one in my family with red hair." I pick up the end and bring it in front of my eyes as if expecting it to change color. "My mom told me I had a recessive gene."

"Hmm, that's interesting. Okay, I need your mom's maiden name and the town she grew up in."

"Her maiden name was Adrianne Marie Helms, and she grew up in Dallas, Texas."

"Perfect, thanks, babe." He takes my hand, and in one motion, he pulls me to my feet. "Let's go for a swim."

"I'm afraid of the water, Anthony. I never go past the point where I can see my toes. There are many things in the ocean that you can't see," I say with concern. "I'll stay here on the beach and watch you swim like I always do." I have stayed out of the water the entire time I've known him.

"I'll take care of you. Come on." He tugs on my arm, trying to drag me toward the water. "If you're going to live at the beach, Em, you're going to have to learn to love the water."

Against my better judgment, I relax and let him take me to the water's edge. I think about the creepy ocean things like sharks and jellyfish as I slowly make my way into the cold saltwater. As soon as I lose sight of my feet, I grab his neck and wrap my legs around his waist. There is no way I'm letting my feet touch the ground. "Don't drop me," I plead.

"I got you. You don't need to be scared," he tells me as I shake in his arms. "You look beautiful with the ocean as your backdrop. Your red hair is blowing in the breeze, and the sun's rays highlight every curve of your body. I get hard just looking at you." His lips touch mine briefly, and his tongue darts out then retreats—he's such a tease.

"Kiss me. Don't tease me, Anthony. I want to feel your lips on me," I beg.

"Oh, you'll feel my lips on you. I plan to taste every inch of your body today. I told you I have an oral fixation." This time, his lips press firmly against mine, and his tongue slides into my mouth as he slowly explores me. I can hardly breathe when he finishes the kiss.

The feel of his erection is no surprise. Anthony has an insatiable sexual appetite. "I gave in and came out here with you, but there is no way I'm having sex in the water."

"No worries, I just wanted to take a quick dip, to relax and enjoy the water. Doesn't it feel great?" His hands grip my ass as he pulls me closer to him. My breasts brush against the hairs on his chest, causing my nipples to pucker and tingle. The sensation makes me squirm ever so slightly. My change in position has him pushing against my entrance. The only things stopping him from full penetration are his shorts and my suit.

"Anthony! What are you doing?" I try to back away from him as I feel one of his fingers slide inside my bathing suit bottom and slip into me. *Oh shit, that feels amazing.* I can't believe how he can turn me on so quickly.

"Stop squirming." He pulls his finger out of me and turns me effortlessly, so I am cradled in his arms. I can feel the length of him against my butt cheeks. "Shall we rinse off?"

"Uh-huh," I respond as I caress his chest and kiss his neck. His muscles are taut from the strain of holding me the last few minutes. I lick the saltwater from that sensitive place that sits between his neck and shoulder. I can hear his breath hitch.

"Let's go inside," he says with some urgency.

We enter the house and go directly to the shower. Setting my feet on the tile floor, he turns on the water. He makes quick work of removing his shorts and my bathing suit.

"Do you want steam, babe?" he asks as he turns on the various showerheads.

"No, it's hot enough just looking at you. Besides, the steam will obstruct my view," I say as I look down at his erection. I lick my lips as I watch it jump in reaction to my gaze.

"I love that tongue of yours and how it darts out of your mouth when you see something you like. I'm glad you like what you see." His eyes roam my body. His fiery gaze lingers at the juncture of my thighs, and he chuckles. "Do you remember when we first started dating, and I told you I wanted to see if you were a natural redhead?" he asks as he looks at my bare mound.

"Yes, and I remember the shocked look on your face when you saw I had no hair. I told you that you would have to take my word for it, but you didn't believe me."

Anthony's hand cups my mound. "I like it," he whispers.

"Mmm." I let out a soft sigh as he pulls his hand from my girlie parts.

"That will be a place where I let my tongue get out of control today." His touch and his words are making me quake with want.

CHAPTER FOUR

Anthony takes my hand and leads me into the shower. The warm water feels nice against my body. Reaching up to the built-in shelf, I grab the bottle of body wash. Bringing it to my nose, I inhale the fresh scent of citrus and squeeze an ample amount into my hand. I rub the gel over my stomach and down my legs.

"Let me do that for you. I will never pass up the opportunity to explore your body." My palms lift off my thighs and are replaced by his strong hands. His touch is sensual and soft. There's a sexual element to it, but it's more than that. It feels like he's studying for a class, and my ass is on the final. He pulls me against his body and holds me. It's the most glorious feeling ever, being held like this as his hands caress my back.

"Ohh," I moan as he massages my skin. My head leans against his chest, and I hear the steady staccato of his heartbeat. We stand like this until our fingers prune before he reaches up and turns off the jets. I follow him out of the shower. Anthony grabs a bath sheet and wraps me like a mummy. I stare at his body and watch his muscles flex as he dries his various parts. I never tire of looking at him. He is no longer erect, but he's still beautiful.

Once dry, he turns his full attention to me. He pulls a smaller towel out of the cupboard and asks me to bend at the waist. I comply and feel him wrap my wet hair in the towel like a turban. Only a man who has been with many women or raised with sisters would know how to do that. Since I know he's an only child, I figure it's the knowledge he's gained from experience. I'm not sure I like that thought.

The bath towel slowly unwinds, exposing my body. He stands in front of me, staring at me as a hungry cat stares at a bird.

"You have an amazing body, Emma. I don't think I will ever get my fill of you."

"So, those runs on the beach are paying off," I say as he leads me to his bed.

"Most definitely." He pulls the blankets back and gestures for me to climb in. I settle myself into the center of the big bed and turn to face him. He lies down beside me, propping up on one elbow to look at me. His lips touch mine, and then he pulls away. I feel him reach up and remove the towel from my head, letting my damp red curls fall around my shoulders.

He draws me to his body and wraps his hand around my back end. His fingers knead my flesh, which sends the fire that he stirs within me straight to my core. My body is aflame with a heated passion that only he has been able to light. I've had a tingle here and there, but I have never had a man release an inferno inside me by a kiss or touch like Anthony does.

"Oh ... Anthony!" I call out as my body pulses with need.

"What do you need, babe? Tell me what you want—what you need."

He rolls me onto my back and lets his fingers glide gently over my body. He hovers at my breasts. My pebbled nipples tingle from the inside out as his lips graze them. I arch up to meet him as he pulls away. I want his mouth on me.

"I need *you*," I pant, hardly able to catch my breath. His warm exhale lingers over my breast before he takes my hard nipple into his mouth. He gently bites down, tugging just before he releases his hold. I swear, there is a direct connection between my nipple and my love nub. I gasp as my sex clenches in reaction.

"You have me, babe. There's no rush; let's enjoy everything. The wait makes the reward that much sweeter." He smiles at me as he moves his body over mine. His oral assault begins at my toes.

"Where did you get this scar from? I've noticed it before but forgot to ask." He rubs the scar that sits smack dab in the middle of my right foot, then focuses his touch on my instep, making me squirm. I try to wriggle my foot away so the ticklish feeling will stop. He pulls back, letting me know he's in charge.

"I'm not completely certain. The lifeguard at Balboa Lagoon said it was probably a stingray barb. I stepped on it while swimming in your beloved ocean. It hurt so much and bled like crazy. I had to have eleven stitches. That's why I'm not too fond of the ocean. You're just walking along, minding your own business—and *bam!* Something reaches up from the murky bottom and takes you out."

His tongue licks warmly over the bottom of my foot, making me twist and turn to free myself. It tickles, and yet the feeling excites me. His mouth slides up my freshly shaved leg and stops at my knee. In one swift move, he turns me over, so my back end is facing the ceiling. His tongue licks the sensitive skin behind my knee and trails up to the top of my thigh. He reaches the area directly under my butt cheek and gently bites. I would've never thought that a tongue sliding from the crack of your bottom to the base of your neck could make you feel so good.

"Mmm," I moan softly as he makes his way from the back of my neck to my ear.

"You're so damn beautiful, and I love the soft moans that escape your mouth when my tongue is on you," he whispers in my ear before he flips me over and crushes his mouth against mine. Just as things heat, he pulls away.

"Where are you going?" I groan. He's driving me insane, taking me to the edge several times without following through. I'm begging for release.

"In good time, baby. I'm enjoying my exploration of your body. I think about it all the time; it's a wonder I get anything done." His eyes look into mine as he lowers his head to the space between my legs. All cohesive thoughts are gone. The minute his lips connect, I am no longer capable of anything.

"Oh ... holy ... hell..." I shout as his tongue thoroughly explores me. Never underestimate a man who tells you he has an oral fixation. The tongue and mouth are two wonders of the world in my book. You can keep the Taj Mahal; I'll take Anthony's tongue any day.

He spends what seems like a lifetime satisfying his need to taste me. As soon as I get close to my climax, he pulls back once more. It's torturous and tantalizing at the same time. As I wriggle under him, he lifts his head. "Now, Emma, come for me," he whispers. And just as he buries his face in my heat, I do. I let loose a scream that could wake the dead. He has taken me to the edge so many times that all of my pent-up energy releases itself in my sex and my scream.

Anthony slowly slides his body up mine. He trails kisses from my stomach to my mouth and settles next to me. I curl into his side, completely satisfied. I look down and see his magnificent erection standing at attention. Gliding my hand down his muscular chest, I follow the trail of brown hair from his belly button to his arousal. Gently holding him in my hand, I begin a slow exploration of his member. Shifting my position, I lower my head so his rock-solid abs support me. He twitches in my hand while I stroke the soft skin that covers his hardness. I watch as a glistening bead escapes the top. Using it as lubrication, I rub my thumb over it, spreading the slick liquid in circles. I firmly but gently wrap my fingers around him and move my fist up and down his shaft in a slow, steady motion. I hear small moans escape his mouth as I change the speed and pressure.

I climb over him and open the drawer to retrieve the lube. I straddle his legs and settle in for playtime. Squeezing an ample amount of lube into my palms, I rub them together to warm things up. *I'm a considerate lover.* There's nothing worse than being all hot and bothered and having your partner put out your flame with ice-cold lube.

I wrap both hands around his girth and move them in opposite directions as I work up and down his length.

"Oh … God, babe, that feels amazing," he groans. I continue to change the pace and pressure, keeping him on edge. As he nears orgasm, I stroke his length with one hand while I gently massage his nipples with the other. Knowing I have him close, I stop everything and lean in for a kiss. I'm learning to play his game.

"You're killing me," he moans as his hands reach for my head to bring me in for a deeper kiss. His talented tongue explores my mouth in slow motion. Everything he does is deliberate. His teeth gently nip at my bottom lip, making me groan in response. I slide back to my straddling position and take him into my hands again. I find a rhythm that has him grinding into my slick palms. His jaw tenses and his teeth clench as he finds his release. His control escapes him with explosive force and lands on his firm stomach. He groans loudly from someplace deep inside. I gently stroke every shudder from his body before I collapse on top of him. His come is slick and warm between our bodies. He holds me tightly as he plays with my hair.

"Shall we take another shower, babe?" he asks.

I snuggle into his shoulder. "Umm-hmm, but can we stay like this for a few minutes? I enjoy being in your arms." He pulls me close to him and places a soft kiss on the top of my head. My heart lurches ever so slightly as I realize I've fallen in love with this man.

"Hey, you fell asleep." He nudges me gently. "Would you like to continue sleeping, or do you want to get up and have a snack with me? I didn't want you waking up alone." There is sweetness in his voice. He is always looking out after me. When I first met him, I thought about his age and figured if he was still single at thirty-four, it was because he was a player or damaged. I still can't figure him out because when I look at him, he's just so perfect. He's almost too good to be true.

CHAPTER FIVE

It's been a week since our relaxing day on the beach. We are standing in his closet, getting dressed to meet our friends at Ahz for dinner. It's been a long week, and we're both ready to unwind and have some fun.

"You know she's going to move in with him, right?" he asks as he buttons his shirt.

"Yeah, I figured as much. I'll have to find a new roommate. Can you zip me up?" I turn around so he can help me into my little black dress.

"Why don't you move in here? You can put your house on the market. You're hardly there, anyway." His hand drops to my lower back, where he gently caresses the area just above my bottom.

I know my eyes must be as big as saucers. "You want me to move in with you?" His expression tells me that this is a serious request. His face is relaxed, but his eyes are watching me intently. "I love that you want me to be with you all the time, but I'm not ready to give up my house. We still stay there sometimes. If I move in here, then I lose a part of me."

I watch as his face falls into a frown. "I don't see you losing a part of you; I see you gaining a part of us. Just think about it, okay?" he asks as he pats me on the bottom.

We pull into the employee garage of Ahz and park in Anthony's designated parking spot. He quickly hops out of the driver's seat and rushes around to open my door.

"It looks like Damon and Kat are already here," I say as I see the silver Mustang parked next to us. "I'm glad that we all meet for dinner at least once a month. Our lives have gotten so busy we hardly get to see each other."

"Are Trevor and Chris joining us tonight as well? We talked about inviting them, but that's all I remember."

"Yes." I look around and see Chris's Volvo parked down the aisle. "They're here as well. That's Chris's Volvo right there." I point to the white car parked three cars away from us. "Are we late? Everyone else is here already." I glance at my watch to check.

"Saving the best for last, babe." He laces his fingers into mine and leads the way into the restaurant.

We enter the Anthony Haywood restaurant on the ground floor and make our way back to the private room that has been set aside for us. I try to stifle a giggle as we wade through the crowded room. It's a busy night at Ahz, and everyone seems to recognize Anthony. It's like Moses parting the Red Sea. People stand aside and let us pass with looks of awe on their faces. I'm not sure if it's because he's the owner or because he's so damn handsome. I watch as every woman he passes undresses him with her eyes. The looks on the faces of the men are pure jealousy; they all wish they were him.

He reaches back and places a possessive hand around my waist. "I hate all these men gawking at you," he grumbles.

I break out into laughter that stops me in my tracks. I force

Anthony to stop when I do. "They aren't staring at me; they wish they were you."

"Exactly, because they know when we go home tonight, it will be me between your legs. I see them all looking at you like they want to devour you. Let's go," he says as he tugs me in his direction again.

"You're crazy. There isn't a man in this room that wants me. I was thinking that every woman in this room is mentally stripping you naked." We finally make it to the back of the restaurant.

Anthony stops before we enter. "I belong to you, babe. And you belong to me. You understand that, right?" He presses his lips to mine in a punishing kiss that leaves me breathless as he opens the door.

Sitting around the round table, I see my friends as I enter the room. I'm still winded by the kiss Anthony gave me and shocked by what he said. That's twice in a week he's claimed me as his own. I think I like that he wants to claim me, but there's also this little alarm going off in my head, telling me to run.

"Well… look who showed up," Kat says. She looks magnificent, and I rush over to her and give her a big hug. I hadn't seen her since the party a week ago.

"You look so pretty." I kiss Kat's cheek, then whisper in her ear, "You look happy. I'm glad you finally came up for air. I've missed you." I pull away and smile at her.

"I'm sorry I missed going to the cemetery with you this year." She wraps her arms around me in a big comforting hug. "I'm sorry we bailed on everyone. I had no idea what was happening, as you know. When he carried me out of the house, we went straight to the airport. We spent the week in Hawaii. We just got back last night."

I smile warmly at my friend. She has been going to the cemetery with me every year since my mom passed away. "It's okay. I went on my own. Anthony wanted to take me, but I wanted to spend some time alone with my thoughts. It worked out."

As Kat reaches up to touch my face, I see a flash of light as her left hand passes by me. "Oh, my God! Is that a ring on your finger?" I squeal. "Why didn't you call me? Best friends are supposed to share shit like this." I grab her hand and look at the biggest diamond I've ever seen.

"It just happened today. Isn't it beautiful?" Kat asks as she holds her hand out for me to see. Her left arm is still in the cast from her car accident, but it doesn't take away from the beauty of her ring. Everyone is now on their feet, surrounding her, everyone but Damon and Anthony; they are standing back, watching us all gush over the news. Damon has the biggest grin on his face.

"Congratulations, guys," I say. "You better treat her right, Damon, or I will hunt you down and hurt you," I threaten playfully.

He walks up to me and kisses me on the cheek. "Emma, I'll love and treasure her for the rest of my life. If I ever hurt her again, I will deliver myself directly to you. You won't even have to hunt me down," Damon says before he grabs his fiancée and takes a seat at the table.

Anthony is sitting to my left, and Kat to my right. Across from me are Chris and Trevor, who are looking quite happy together. "Hey Chris, how are things at the bank?" I ask.

"Good. I have this new client that comes every day at noon to make a deposit." He looks up at Trevor with a glimmer in his eyes. "He's my favorite." His directness used to shock me when I was a kid.

I spent my teenage years with Kat and her family. They are direct—beyond direct. Their entire family lacks filters. You're forced to engage with them, or you get left behind. Living with the Cross family was probably my saving grace. They were a real family. In time, they became my family. Chris is Kat's brother, and Trevor is his partner. Trevor fits right in with the group.

Trevor does something to Chris under the table because suddenly, Chris lets out a yelp. Everyone at the table looks at him and laughs.

"Okay, apparently I'm going to have to find a new roommate, so I'm counting on you guys to send me the perfect replacement for Kat."

"You're going to replace me?" Kat asks. Her lips purse into the perfect-looking pout.

"Well, it's not like you're going to move back in. You live in a mansion in the hills with your hunky fiancé," I tease. "You know I can never replace you; you're my sister from another mister." I stick my tongue out at her. "So, when is the big day? I'm your maid of honor, right? I can't see Chris or Trevor looking good in a bridesmaid gown."

"I'll have you know, I look lovely in satin," Trevor says.

Kat looks at both of us before she speaks. "No date yet, and only girls with vaginas can wear dresses at my wedding."

We talk for a few minutes to catch up. The server takes our order and pours us all a glass of red wine. It's nice to be together. I love all these people. Trevor is a recent addition, but the way he looks at Chris makes me happy. Chris is like my flesh and blood, and it's important to me he has someone who loves and values him. We've paired up quite nicely. Looking around at the people surrounding me, I know there is nowhere I'd rather be. I stand up to make a toast.

"To all of us who love, may we love deeply." Everyone clinks their glasses together and shouts out loud, "Hear, hear."

We spend the next hour chatting, eating, and drinking wine. Anthony orders some type of flaming dessert to celebrate Kat and Damon's engagement. The conversation goes back to my need for a new housemate.

"Em, I know a girl you might want to talk to," Trevor says. I watch as he whispers into Chris's ear. Both of them nod their heads. "There's this girl that works as a bartender at Trax," Trevor begins. "We kind of adopted her. She makes good money, has a great personality, and we like her. She was saying last week that she wants to find someplace to live that's closer to work. She could be a good fit." Trevor seems pleased to contribute a solution to my dilemma.

"Okay, give her my number." I feel Anthony place his hand on my thigh and give it a gentle squeeze.

"If Emma would just move in with me, she wouldn't need to find a new roommate." I swing around to look at him. "Don't give me that look," he says. "These are our friends, and I need them to help put the pressure on you so I can get my way."

I examine everyone at the table and notice that they are staring at me, waiting for a response. "Anthony asked me to move in with him today. I'm considering his offer since I pretty much live with him, anyway." I pucker my lips and touch them to Anthony's quickly before continuing. "I'm not ready to let go of my house, though, so regardless of my decision, I will need a renter."

"What happened to us, man?" Damon looks at Anthony as he asks the question. "A few months ago, we were confirmed bachelors." He reaches over and picks up Kat's hand. "This one stole my heart, and it looks like you're in just as bad a shape as I am."

"Don't I know it? My heart doesn't beat unless she's near me. That's why I want her to move in. Is it selfish that I want to live?" Anthony says as he looks at me with pouty lips and puppy dog eyes.

"Oh...my...God. You guys are relentless. Okay, I'll move in with you, but I'm not selling my house." I let out an exasperated breath of air.

Before I know it, I'm no longer sitting in my seat. Anthony has catapulted me into his arms and is swinging me around. I've never seen him so happy. "I love you," he whispers in my ear. "We're picking up your things on our way home."

We leave the get-together and drive straight to my house. It doesn't take us long to throw a bunch of my clothes and shoes in his car. Once his little car is full, we race home.

I lie in bed and wait for Anthony to lock up the house and come downstairs.

The layout of his house is interesting. The main floor contains an amazing gourmet kitchen with all the bells and whistles, a living room, and a dining room. There are also three bedrooms, three bathrooms, and an office on that floor. A wall of windows opens to a deck that overlooks the water. The panels slide into the wall and disappear. When we have them open, the house is completely exposed to the elements. There is a recreation room and spectacular master suite that opens to the beach on the lower level.

"What are you thinking about?" Anthony asks, sneaking up and startling me.

"I was thinking about my new house. I'm so glad it comes with a cook and a housekeeper." The wink of my left eye puts a smile on his face.

"Well, your cook and housekeeper require compensation. I think that a naked redhead in my bed every night might be worth the extra laundry. I think if she strips down the minute she walks into the house every day, I'd vacuum and dust as well."

"I didn't know you were so cheap and easy." I toss off the sheet, exposing my upper body. "If I knew that showing you these," I grab my breasts and lift them, "or this," I toss the sheet and cup my sex, "would get me so much attention, I might have negotiated earlier."

"You have always had my attention. I remember the first day I saw you. You were at the food and wine festival with that food critic, Blake Havers. I watched you that afternoon and thought you were his girlfriend. I couldn't figure out how you would be attracted to him. He's such a slimy little worm. I hadn't even met you, but I wanted you then." Taking off his tie, he places it on the chair in the corner of the room and sits down to remove his shoes. "I asked around and found out you were an escort. My first thought was a prostitute because honestly, you're the only girl I know of who runs an actual legitimate escort service." He sets his shoes and discarded socks next to the chair.

"Do you know many girls who run an escort service?" My eyes narrow at him. *Just how many escorts does he know?*

"I know a few. Remember, I've been hanging out with Damon for years." His shoulders shake as he laughs. "Damon is the one who cleared everything up for me. I was asking him to give me the number for the pretty redheaded escort I'd seen him with. I wanted to get laid. He said he didn't know a pretty redheaded escort that offered those services. I described you, and then he figured it out. That's when I got your number, and I called you for the fundraiser."

"So, he knew you were going to call me for that fundraiser. No wonder he folded so easily when I asked him to take Kat. That *shit*, he was matchmaking. Just wait until I see him again." I roll onto my side so I can see Anthony.

"What are you going to do? Thank him? If he hadn't graciously bowed out, I'd still be wondering who that redheaded girl was, and you never would've heard my voice over the phone."

"True. The minute I heard your voice, I knew I had to make it work out. I've never had my body quiver from a man's voice, but I drenched my panties the day you called. I googled you the minute we got off the phone. One look at your picture, and I was hooked."

"I picked that dress out specifically for you. I wanted to make sure you remembered who I was." I'd never worn that blue dress before. It was cut in a V down the front and the back to my navel and my bottom. It was very provocative.

"That dress was criminal; I don't know how you kept your girls from falling out. I was mesmerized. I'm still mesmerized by them." He walks over to me and places a soft kiss on each of my nipples, making them perk up as if reaching for his mouth. He unbuttons his shirt as I watch with rapt attention. "You teased me all night and then told me you didn't mix business with pleasure." He makes a *tsk tsk* sound as he peels off his shirt.

"You fired me, marched me out the front door, and tossed me into a cab," I say with some indignation.

"I fired you and told you I'd pick you up the next night for a date. I kissed you before I gently placed you into the cab. It seems as if we have a different recollection of the events leading up to us."

"I believe you have the more accurate recollection," I confess. Hearing his version of our story makes me laugh. It's not that we haven't talked about it before, but each time we revisit our beginning, he always paints a prettier story for himself.

"I went home with the most painful hard on that night. I hardly slept, thinking of all the ways I could pleasure you. When I arrived to pick you up, you were beautiful in your sundress and sandals. I knew I wasn't bringing you home that night. However, I never thought we would be here, in this place right now. I never thought I could want a woman as much as I want you. Sometimes it scares the hell out of me, Emma. I let you into my heart, and now you own it. You have the power to crush my soul."

Oh, my goodness, did my heart leap? "I love you, Anthony. You're an amazing man. Do you realize you're my actual first boyfriend?"

The look of surprise flashed in his expressive eyes. "Surely, that's not true. You have dated people before." He unbuttons and unzips his slacks and lets them fall to the floor. Picking them up, he folds them as he walks back to the chair.

"I never had a boyfriend. In high school, I used a lot of boys to fill the gaps in my life. Kat's mom had a long talk with me about respecting my body and myself. She put me in counseling, and I changed my ways. By the time I graduated, I had to support myself. I started doing the companion thing and had little time to date. I saw someone regularly a few years ago, but he couldn't handle my job. There was an altercation. I got in the middle of it and ended up with a black eye. As you might imagine, I don't have any tolerance for aggression or physical violence."

"Someone hit you?" he yells. He races to the bed and clasps my arms in his hands. "I'll kill him. Who the hell hit you?" His face is red, and the little vein on his forehead is pulsing.

"Calm down. He didn't try to hit me; I stepped in between him and my client. When Mark threw the punch, I was in the way. It was an accident, but I never saw him again. He let jealousy get the best of him. The funny thing is nothing had happened. My client was walking me up the stairs to my house, and he put his hand on my back to guide me. Mark didn't like seeing another man's hands on me. It was stupid."

"Not to defend a man who hit you, but I wouldn't want to see another man touch you. It irks me when I catch someone looking at you."

"You are so funny. No one is looking at me except for you. Come here and make love to me." I lean across the bed and take his hand in mine. I pull his body down to lie beside me. His dark-chocolate brown curls frame his face perfectly. Even though his hair has a mind of its own, it seems to fall effortlessly in place.

We are silent as we explore each other's bodies. The anticipation is building as our hands become bolder, and our need becomes stronger. He rolls my nipples between his fingertips. The sensation stirs the warmth between my legs. I have been waiting all night to feel him sink himself into my body. His fingers make their way slowly down my stomach and find their way to my hot center. He gently slides his fingers down my moist folds, peeling back the layers to get to my center. I swell from the passion that's building; my body opens like a flower. Each time he crosses my opening, he dips his fingers inside of me to grab the moisture that's building. I writhe under his touch and grind myself against him. My free hands go to work, trying to bring him to the point where I am—a place that no matter what we do, everything feels fantastic. I want him to feel as good as I do.

He is firm in my hand, and I glide my palm up and down his length. I am rewarded with a guttural moan. As I bring the fingers of my free hand to his chest, I graze his nipple. I am then rewarded with a growl. I push him to his back and straddle him.

"I'm taking control, Anthony. Lay back and enjoy baby," I say as I lower myself onto his length. The feeling takes my breath away. I moan with pleasure as he fills me. I slowly raise and lower my body until we are both breathless. His hands caress my breasts as I lean into his touch. I feel his body shift. He turns us around without breaking contact or missing a beat. I now lay beneath him. He pounds out a steady rhythm that brings me to the edge. I reach down to touch myself, knowing that a few strokes of my finger will get me to the place I want to go. He reaches for both of my legs and pulls them to his shoulders. He is now wholly inside in me. I feel him hit the deepest part of me. His mouth is slightly open, and he tilts his head back. If I had to describe ecstasy, I would describe his face at this exact moment. I continue to rub myself as he hammers into me. The telling tingle starts in my nipples and slowly seeps down my spine until my body shatters. I scream out his name as I throb around him.

"*Oh… God!*" he calls out. He lets my legs fall and collapses on top of me. I feel the pulse of his release as he empties himself into me. I drag my fingertips lightly across his back as he lets out a contented "Mmm."

CHAPTER SIX

I wake to the sound of waves crashing against the shore. There is a chill in the air that sends me searching for Anthony's warm body. My hand blindly reaches for him in the darkened room, but I find nothing. The spot where he lay last night is empty and cold. I open my eyes and scan the room to find he's gone. The thought saddens me. My favorite part of the morning is waking up next to him.

The door leading to the beach is slightly ajar, allowing the cool morning air to enter. I watch the curtains as they billow in the breeze. Sliding slowly from the bed, I put on my robe before opening the door fully. I peek my head outside and see a lone swimmer. I can't be sure, but I think it's Anthony. I watch as he rounds the buoy and makes his way back to shore. He battles the break of the water to emerge, god-like, out of the ocean. Poseidon comes to mind as I watch the water drip off his broad shoulders. Shoulders formed by hours of swimming. Anthony's Triton sits between his legs instead of carrying it in his hand.

With a shake of his head, the water splashes in all directions before his locks fall perfectly around his face. I take in the sight of him as he walks to me. His blue swim trunks hang low on his hips, and I devour his body with my eyes. His solid abs blend into the perfect V that disappears into his navy-blue swim shorts.

"Hey, Emma, I thought you would've slept longer. I figured I had enough time for a quick swim before I woke you up. I was going to bring you breakfast in bed."

His smile melts my insides. What do you say to a gorgeous man that wants to serve you breakfast in bed? "I just got up. I can run back and climb into bed if you want me to," I tease.

He laughs as he pulls me by the hand and drags me into the bathroom, leaving a trail of sand in his wake. He wastes no time divesting me of my robe. "Let's jump in the shower. When we're finished, I'll make you a killer breakfast while you keep me company."

There is no invite or question, just a directive from a man who's used to getting his way. I don't typically answer to men, but having spent the last few months with Anthony, I'm getting used to his bossiness. It's not an entirely unpleasant experience. I certainly wouldn't be comfortable submitting to a man regularly, but Anthony and I seem to have found a good balance.

"Where are you, Emma? You seem to be deep in thought," he inquires as he lathers up my body.

"I was thinking about how bossy you are. I thought it would bother me at first, but it's been nice to depend on someone." I take the bath gel and reciprocate, slowly running my hands along his body. I love the feel of him under my palms. I ask him to turn around so I can wash his back. My ulterior motive is to see his backside. He has the nicest—rock-solid—back end I've ever laid eyes on. I lean my body against him, kissing his shoulder blade, and wrap my arms around his waist. His hands fold over mine as we stand like this for few moments. Turning around, he picks me up. I wrap my legs around his waist, feeling his hardness against my bottom. Our eyes connect before our lips. The kiss is swoon worthy. I can feel his passion flow through me as our tongues collide together. My eyes look to his and find the look of fierce passion and need. His tongue darts out of his mouth, licking his lips. I'm getting to learn his mannerisms, and I think this one means *I'm hungry for you.*

He turns off the shower jets with one hand. Never letting my feet touch the floor, he carries my dripping body to bed. I giggle as he throws me to the center and tickles me.

"I love your laugh, Emma. It warms my heart to hear you so carefree." He stops for a minute and looks at me seriously. "Thank you for moving in with me, babe. I know it was a hard decision, but I am glad it ended up in my favor."

He settles himself between my legs, and that's where he stays for the rest of the morning.

I don't get my breakfast in bed, but I'm not disappointed. Anthony and I emerge from our bedroom late in the morning to eat breakfast together on the deck. We settle for fresh fruit and bagels and a fantastic cup of coffee.

"What should I wear to your parents' house tonight? I'm nervous about meeting them. This will be my first meet-the-parents experience." I pop a juicy strawberry into my mouth. One perk of dating a master chef is that you get the best produce available.

"Wear whatever you feel comfortable in. It's a casual dinner, so you can wear jeans if you want. My parents are going to love you. This is a fairly new experience for all of us. I've only brought one girl home before you. I guess my parents will be just as nervous as you are."

"You lucked out, never having to meet my parents. I wish my mom could've met you, though. She would've liked you."

"I met the Crosses at your graduation, and they gave me the third degree. They stepped right into the parent role for you. Speaking of parents, I hired an investigator to look around Dallas for me. I have plans to visit the locations we have there in a couple of weeks. I'm hoping he'll have something for me then."

"What do you think you're going to find?"

"Probably nothing. I'll most likely learn that your dad is just an asshole, but if I can learn something different, then I plan to keep looking. I found something interesting, though. I was going to wait to say something." He looks over his coffee cup as he takes a sip. "I sent for your parents' marriage license and your birth certificate. It turns out they married only months before you were born."

I'm speechless. I never knew when my parents got married. I had no reason to ask because they never celebrated an anniversary. I just assumed that they did it like most people in their generation did. You met, you fell in love, and you married. Nine months later, your bundle of joy is born, and everyone lives happily ever after. Well, I know the happily ever after was bullshit. They didn't have a loving marriage. I feel like I'm being sucked into some black hole. My head spins, and everything fades when I realize I'm holding my breath. As soon as I release it and breathe in, everything rights itself.

"Em, are you okay? I'm assuming by your reaction you didn't know. I'm sorry. Maybe I should have kept that information to myself." His thumb and index finger begin a slow circular motion as he rubs his temples.

I pucker my lips and exhale; the sound that comes out is more like a whistle. "No, it's okay. I guess it answers a few questions. He married my mom because he knocked her up. Being Catholic, you didn't get pregnant before you were married. That would explain why he hated me. Most men would hate to be roped into a marriage." I rub my face with my hands, trying to digest this recent information. "Wow, you just confirmed what I always knew. I'm no one's love child. I'm more of an 'oops.'"

Anthony moves over to my chaise lounge, lifts me, and puts me in his lap. "You're my love child. Most kids are more like an 'oops' if their parents are honest. I know I was. Are you going to be okay?" He turns my head so he can see my eyes. "Should I call off the detective? I don't want to hurt you with information like this."

"You're not hurting me. The hurt I feel was done a long time ago."

"Okay, but why do you think she stayed with him? Did you ever ask her?"

I contemplate this for a moment. I do remember my mom telling me that marriage in God's eyes was for life. "Being raised Catholic, you married and stayed married. My mom was a devout parishioner. She would drag me to church every week my dad was gone. When he was home, she didn't leave the house."

"So... you're Catholic." It's more of a statement than a question.

"No, I'm nothing. I stopped going to church when my mom passed away. I couldn't believe anymore. How can you justify a god that overlooks the things that happened in my family?" I look down at my index finger as it draws invisible circles on Anthony's leg. "Where was he when my mom was getting her ass beat? Is it fate, karma, or God? I have no idea. I like to believe that the universe has a plan, but I'm not sure."

"My family wasn't big into going to church. I think I went to a few Christmas services, but the only time I step into a church is for a wedding, a funeral, or a christening."

"Speaking of weddings, did it surprise you that Damon proposed to Kat?" I know I was shocked, so it will be interesting to see Anthony's take on things.

"No, I saw him at the party where he won her back. I also saw how miserable he was without her. It doesn't surprise me at all. He's taking no chances that she will get away again. I'm surprised he didn't kidnap her and take her to Vegas for a quickie marriage in a drive-thru chapel," he jokes.

"I can't imagine Kat getting married in a drive-thru chapel. I'd do that, but there's no way she would." Standing up to stretch, I walk to the rail and look out over the water. "She'll have the whole church wedding, long white dress thing. I bet her mom is over the moon.

She likes Damon." The wind is kicking up, making the waves crash harder on the sand.

"He's quite a catch. Who wouldn't want a handsome and rich son-in-law?" he asks as he comes to stand behind me.

"I guess if that's important to you. Not everyone likes rich, handsome men." I turn around and poke him playfully in the chest. "Take me, for example. I like old men because I chose someone who's ten years my senior to fall in love with." I cover my mouth quickly like my statement just slipped out.

CHAPTER SEVEN

"You did not just call me old and use the word 'senior' in the same sentence. I know I must have heard you wrong." He gives me a serious look. His eyes narrow, and his head tilts, adding intensity to his stare down.

I look around for an escape. He has me caged between his arms and the deck rail, but I duck under him and make a run for the stairs. I make it to the bottom when I feel him grab the tie to my robe. In one yank, the robe is gone. I am free, but I am naked. I continue to run from him, knowing that eventually, he will catch me, but until he does, I will continue to taunt him.

"See, you must be old because you can't even catch me. My twenty-four-year-old body has outsmarted and outpaced you, old man." I have now trapped myself between him and the water. He knows I won't go into the ocean on my own, so he slows things down and stalks me.

"You know, babe, when I catch you, I am going to show you how old I am. What I can't finish before we leave for my parents, I'll pick up after we return. I'm going to make you eat those words," he threatens. I'm winded from the chase, but he isn't even breathing hard.

"You'll have to catch me first." I make a break for it but get caught in his grip, trying to run past him. We both fall onto the sand in a fit of laughter. I'm stark naked, and he is barely wrapped in his robe. Shrugging it off, he pins me to the ground with his body.

"Does this feel like a man who's old?" he asks as he pushes his hardness against my side. He leans to his left, keeping me pinned in place by his hip and leg. His right hand comes up to brush the hair from my face.

"You're in good shape for an older guy," I say, trying to squirm away from him. It's an exercise in futility. He has me, and he will not let me go.

"Let me show you what this older guy is capable of," he says as he gently kisses my lips.

I wasn't expecting this kind of tenderness after all the teasing I did. I relax and melt into the sand as he places short, sweet kisses across my lips. His hand slides up from my hip to softly cup the swell of my breast. Feeling his touch sends a frizzle of excitement through me. I open my mouth to sigh. He takes full advantage of that as his tongue slides past my lips. There is a complete exploration before the dueling of our tongues begins. The kiss lasts for an eternity; its intensity brings a fire to the pit of my stomach. Everything for me starts with either a heart-squeezing moment or a thigh-clenching moment. Today's events are wreaking havoc between my legs.

"Do you like this, babe?" he asks as his hand begins to squeeze gently.

"Uh... huh..." I hum, barely able to catch my breath. He's got me panting and at his mercy.

His hand leaves my breast and slowly slides down my stomach. It takes up residence between my legs. As his fingers work their magic, a soft moan escapes my lips. "Mmm."

"Does this feel good, babe?" he asks as he slides a finger inside of me.

"Ohh… mmm… hmm," I reply.

He's strategic, touching me in precisely the right place, with the right amount of pressure to take me soaring to the top. Just as I begin to feel the first shudder of my release, he pulls back, plummeting me back to Earth. He continues his relentless teasing until I am begging him for my release.

"Do you want to come, Em? Are you ready?" he whispers seductively in my ear.

"Yes! I want to come, Anthony…take me there," I beg.

He lifts his head and devours me with his eyes. The intensity of his stare almost takes me over the top. His body shifts and I spread my legs, waiting for him to take his place between them. When I think he's going to plunge himself deep inside me, he rises to his feet, grabs his robe, and heads indoors.

"Let's go, babe. We have to be at my parents' house in an hour." I can hear his laughter from the house as he disappears inside.

I can't believe he just did that to me. He knew what he was doing. Now I'm going to have to spend the evening in a body that's in a heightened, sexually aroused state. My skin is hypersensitive, my nipples tingle, and I can't stop squeezing my thighs together. *Oh, I'm a mess.* I tilt my head back to see if he's gone into the house before I let out a scream.

I pull myself up off the sand and walk into our bedroom. He is just stepping out of the shower. One look at him, and I am back in a state of arousal.

"Do you want me to turn the shower on for you?" he asks.

I walk my naked body past him, making sure I brush him with my breasts as I pass. "No, I got it," I say. I step into the shower and turn on the nozzles. I see him watching me in the mirror as he shaves. Two can play at this game. I don't even have to touch him to get him all worked up.

I take the shower gel off the shelf and squeeze it into my hand. Standing directly in front of the door where Anthony will get the best view, I sensually wash my body and let my hands linger on his favorite parts while he watches from the mirror. I turn around and give him a view of his most favorite part of me—my backside. I hear him groan as I slowly bend over and push my bottom against the shower door.

"What are you doing, Em?"

"Just shaving my legs, baby. I'm trying to hurry," I purr while I wag my tail end back and forth. When I finish my task, I turn around and see he has left the room. A giggle escapes me.

Once I exit the shower and dry off, I run my fingers through my curls and decide to let my hair air dry. I apply a small amount of foundation, just enough to cover the freckles that pepper my nose. After three coats of mascara, a sweep of blush, and a bit of lip gloss, I'm ready to get dressed. The closet has a few of my things in it. I plan to take up the left side of the large walk-in, leaving the right to him. I think he might have as many clothes as I do. Deciding on a black and white sundress and ballet flats, I quickly get dressed and go in search of my man.

I find him leaning over the rail in the exact location we started this cat-and-mouse routine. I walk up behind him and put my arms around his waist.

"Are you ready to go?" A big smile breaks across his face as he turns around and sees me. "You look amazing, Em. Good enough to eat."

"Oh... don't start with me again. I'm still tittering on edge from your little game earlier," I tell him. I look toward the sandy area where we'd lain and feel my insides tighten as I remember how close I got to ecstasy.

"My game? Who started this game, young lady? If I recall correctly, you called me an old man, and I fully intend to show you how young and virile I am." He puffs out his chest as if that is going to convince me he's young and potent. I wouldn't be surprised if he started beating on it like an ape.

"You know I was teasing you. I already know how virile you are." I reach forward and cup him, giving him a gentle squeeze. "I've never been with anyone as sexy as you, baby."

I watch as his head rolls back, and he breathes deep. "You're killin' me, Red. Grab your bag and let's go before I call my parents and tell them something came up." He looks down at his increasing arousal. Taking my hand from his pants, he pulls me toward the garage.

We both get in the Vanquish, and he turns to me. "You've wheedled your way into my heart, and you've taken over my mind. I used to have some control over my dick, but even that's gone. You control it all. What do you have to say for yourself, you little vixen?"

I contemplate my answer for a minute as he pulls out of the garage and drives us toward Hollywood.

"I couldn't find my underwear," I reply as a huge smile takes over my face.

CHAPTER EIGHT

Forty minutes later, we pull up in front of a small bungalow that looks very similar to my house. It's an older neighborhood but well-maintained, with a brick walkway curving to the front. Several varieties of roses are planted next to the walkway, giving the home a cottage feel.

Anthony exits the car and comes around to help me out. I have to remember to tell his mom thank you for teaching him such excellent manners. We walk hand in hand to the door, making one stop on the way so I can smell the yellow roses. As I bend over, I feel his hand rub against my bottom as if he's checking to see if I was telling him the truth.

"I already told you I didn't wear any. When are you going to believe me?" I shake my head at him and roll my eyes skyward.

"You are in so much trouble when we get home. You realize that, right?"

"Can't wait, baby, I love punishment sex. That's what you're talking about, right? Hard and fast? No mercy? I'm counting on it." I leave him alone with a shocked look on his face. He races up the stairs, catching up with me on the porch.

The door swings open before he can respond. I turn my smile to the woman standing in front of me.

"Oh, my goodness, this must be Emma. Come in, sweetheart. Anthony, why did you keep her waiting on the porch? We saw you drive up a few minutes ago. What were you doing out here for so long?"

"Hey, Mom. Emma was smelling your flowers." He leans over and kisses his mom on her cheek.

"Do you like roses, Emma? I have ten different varieties planted out there. You should see them in June; they are all in full bloom, and the whole yard smells heavenly." She closes her eyes and inhales as if she can smell the flowers from memory.

"Yes, Mrs. Haywood, I love roses. They remind me of my mother. She also had a love for them. Her favorite was the Julia Child rose. It looks very similar to the yellow rose you have planted down the walkway. It's one of the most fragrant roses I've ever smelled." I point to the center of the walkway, where the big yellow blooms are located.

"That's exactly what that is. I bought that at a garden show about ten years ago when Anthony opened his first restaurant. It's taken off, just like his career. Make sure I clip off some flowers for you to take home today, and Emma, please call me Claire."

"Mom, do you want to stand on the porch all evening and talk about flowers, or should we go in?" Anthony asks.

"Of course, I won't make you wait out here. Come on in and have a seat. I want to hear all about you," Claire says. She takes my hand and pulls me into the living room.

I follow her to the couch, where she gestures for me to sit. As I survey the room, I notice that all the furniture is upholstered in a floral print. It's sweet, in a grandma kind of way. The curtains are lace sheers with one of those fluffy valances on the top. I haven't seen anything like it since I was a kid.

"Thanks for having me over, Mrs... I mean, Claire. I've been looking forward to meeting you."

"Of course, we're so pleased to have you join us for dinner. Anthony, tell your father Emma is here," she says. Claire is wearing a blue chambray shirtdress and sensible loafers. She could've escaped straight out of the television show *Leave It To Beaver*. She's like an updated June Cleaver.

I look at Anthony; my eyes are pleading with him not to leave me alone. As he steps behind his mother, I watch him break out into a silent laugh. *Oh... I'm going to make him pay for this.*

"Anthony says that you live with him now." She walks over and sits down beside me. "You know, in my day, you didn't try it before you buy it. You just signed on the dotted line, and you committed for life. Society is much more forgiving today than it was years ago."

What am I supposed to say to that? I opt to ignore her statement and move along. "How long have you and Mr. Haywood been married?" That should buy me some time.

"Let's see... we met when I was eighteen, and we married when I was twenty. I'm fifty-eight, so that would make thirty-eight years."

"That's marvelous. Congratulations."

"David is older than me by eight years. I like an older man; I assume you do as well. Isn't my Anthony older than you?" She smiles at me, and I can see Anthony gets his smile from her. She has beautiful straight white teeth and full lips that break into a full grin.

"Yes, he's ten years older than me." Claire reaches under the table and brings out what looks like a photo album.

"I think an older man is good. They take a while to mature. Come closer. I want to show you, Anthony, when he was a boy." I move in, so we are side by side. Looking over the three-inch-thick album, I realize it's going to be a long evening. "Why don't you look at these while I check on dinner? Can I bring you something to drink?" She rises from the sofa and walks across the room.

"I've got it, Mom," Anthony says as he returns from who knows where. Walking a few steps behind him is his dad. He enters the living room with a glass of red wine in each hand. Anthony is the spitting image of his father; he'll be an incredibly handsome older man. I'll have to tell him later when we talk about his age again.

"Emma, this is my dad, David. Dad, this is my Emma." Anthony sits beside me and passes me a glass of wine.

He called me *his* Emma. I'd fall over and faint if I had panties on. I can't risk my dress floating up, so I guess I'll have to settle for the warm fuzzy feeling I have in my chest. His hand travels down my back and comes to rest against my bottom. His touch sends a chill up my spine.

"It's nice to meet you, Emma. Anthony has been telling us how he's met an extraordinary girl. All I have to say is, it's about time." His dad takes a seat across from me. "I see Claire has given you the album of shame. She loves to show that book off to Anthony's girlfriends; unfortunately, he's only brought one home before you." Anthony gives his dad a sideways glance.

I open the book to the first page and see the cutest baby I've ever seen. Looking up at Anthony, he almost looks embarrassed. "You were so cute."

"What do you mean *were*?" He gives me the evil eye.

"Now you're the most handsome man, but you were a darling baby." I lean over and kiss his cheek. Claire enters the room and sits on the other side of me. I'm officially the center of a Haywood sandwich.

"Wasn't he the cutest thing? We tried for four years to conceive, but nothing. I enrolled in secretarial school, and bang—I was pregnant."

I look toward Anthony and watch as he mouths the word "oops."

I flip through the pages and see him as a boy growing up. He was a very active kid; there are pictures of him playing soccer, baseball, and football—the photos chronicle his life. He ages every few pages. The high school pictures are so funny. "Wow, you had braces? What grade were you in when this was taken?" I ask, pointing at the image on the right.

"I was in ninth grade, I think." The picture staring back at me is a pimply-faced kid with a tin grin.

"Well, I'd have been getting ready to enter kindergarten the year after they took this." I giggle as I try to keep a straight face. He gives me a pinch on my bottom, making me jump a little in my seat. The next page shows him in a tux. As I look at the picture, I see he had red Chucks peeking out from the bottom of his black tuxedo pants. Next to him is a pretty blonde girl. "Junior Prom?" I ask.

"Yes, and before you ask, my date's name was Sabrina. We had a couple of dates, and that's it."

"I wasn't going to ask." I turn the page and find a picture of him with shoulder-length hair and a surfboard tucked under his arm. "Oh, my God, you were a surfer dude. Now I understand your love of the ocean."

"He's been in the ocean since he could swim. He used to compete in surfing competitions when he was younger. He gave that up when he gave Rose up. He'll have to show you his collection of trophies," Claire says.

"Rose? This is the first time I've heard of Rose." I look up at Anthony with a questioning look. I watch as his body stiffens. Why does this Rose girl cause such a reaction?

"She's no one. We dated for a while, and then we didn't." He tries to roll over the subject as if it never existed.

I turn to the last page and find another formal picture. This time he had purple Chucks to match his purple bowtie and cummerbund. It reminds me of the tux he wore for the opening of Ahz, only he wore nice Italian leather shoes instead. Next to him is a leggy blonde. "Looks like you had a thing for blondes."

"That was before I found out that redheads were so much more fun. When do I get to see pictures of your prom dates?" he asks.

"Never. I didn't go to prom." There is a gasp throughout the room. Everyone looks stunned that I didn't partake in the whole prom experience.

"I can't believe that a girl as pretty as you didn't get asked to prom," David says.

"I got asked. I didn't attend."

Claire pats me on the shoulder as if to say I'm sorry. "Anthony, why don't you take Emma on the grand tour of our mansion." She looks at me and rolls her eyes. "Don't forget to show her your trophy room. I'm going to check on dinner." David and Claire walk out of the room, leaving Anthony and me alone.

"Ready to see my bedroom, Em?" He takes my hand and helps me into a standing position. His lips meet mine as his hand drops to caress my bottom. I can feel him pulling my dress up to cop a feel. I quickly pull it down and step away from him.

"Stop, your mom and dad could walk in at any minute," I chastise him.

He gives me the same smile I saw in his photos from high school. "Let's go, babe. I want you to see what a stud I was." He takes me by the hand and leads me down a hallway covered with pictures from kindergarten to graduation. "Close your eyes," he says before he opens the door that takes us back to his youth. I do as he asks. Guiding me into his room, he grabs my waist and sits me on something soft that I assume is his bed. I feel him move away from me. I hear the door close and the unmistakable click of a lock. There is a rustling of what sounds like papers.

"Can I open my eyes?" My heart races. I know he's up to something.

"No," he says. I keep my eyes closed and sit patiently.

"What are you doing, baby? Your mom is going to be looking for us soon." I can feel the air change in the room. There is a crackle of energy in the atmosphere. Sensing him in front of me, I reach out. His hands settle on my knees, making my skin tingle as his fingers slide up my inner thighs. I feel as if I may implode. His fingers reach the apex of my thighs, his thumbs glide in and spread me apart. I lie back and allow my legs to fall open, giving in. I need this. He has been stoking and banking my fire all day. His hot velvet tongue strokes me, and I claw at the bedding and bite my lips shut. Just as I am about to explode, he pulls back.

"Oh...God...please don't do this to me again. I swear I don't think you're old. I was teasing. I love everything about you, baby. Please don't leave me like this," I beg.

"The thought of you sitting here bare under your dress is driving me crazy. If you ever tell me you are pantiless again, I will take you wherever we are. Do you understand? You can't play that game with me and not expect me to respond."

His head drops to my mouth to catch the frustrated scream that threatens to escape. I pull my legs up around his waist, trying to pull him closer to me. I dig my nails into his shoulders, clawing at any relief I can get.

"I've had a lot of fantasies in this room, but making love to you on my twin bed would beat them all. What do you say?"

"Your mom and dad are in the next room," I answer with alarm. I need a release, but I know myself, and quiet isn't part of my sexual vocabulary.

He sighs heavily before he straightens me up and pulls me into a sitting position. I will have to stay in my sexually heightened state for a while longer. I exhale and open my eyes.

"Holy smokes—you have at least a hundred trophies in here." There isn't a surface in his room that's not covered with a trophy or medal of some sort. On the desk are several photos that are turned upside down. I wonder if that's the rustling of papers that I heard.

"What can I say? I'm an overachiever." He smiles smugly.

"Why did you make me close my eyes?"

"I didn't want you to get overwhelmed by my greatness," he teases as he looks around his room. His eyes settle on the photos on the desk.

"Who's in the photos?"

He looks at me sheepishly. "Just some girl I dated. My mom still had her pictures pinned to my corkboard, and I wanted to remove them before you saw them. It's just someone from my distant past, and I don't want to talk about her."

"Okay, I understand totally." I look around the room again. I won't pry into what he doesn't want me to see.

"Is this what your room was like when you were a kid?"

"Exactly, except I had a pile of dirty clothes in the corner, and it smelled like sweat instead of your arousal. I like this smell so much better." He plants a quick kiss on my lips. "Shall we join my parents?"

I growl in frustration as he guides me out of his room and into the dining room. My parts are still tingling. It's almost cruel how he takes me to the point of no return and then makes a U-turn to deliver me back to ground zero.

We sit down to dinner with his parents. Claire and David sit at the ends of the dining room table, and Anthony and I flank both sides. I wait to see how to progress with dinner, not sure if they say a blessing. I look across the table and smile as Anthony winks at me.

"Guests first. Emma, please help yourself," Claire says. "I'm not a fancy cook like Anthony, but I make a good meatloaf. I hope you like it." I carefully scoop up a slice of mystery loaf, a spoonful of mashed potatoes, and pass the plate to my right.

"I love meatloaf. My mom used to make it when I was a young girl. It was different every time. I used to call it mystery loaf because you never knew what it would taste like, but it was always good. This is comfort food to me."

David piles his food high on his plate. "How did you meet Anthony?" he turns to me and asks.

"Yeah, babe, how did we meet?" Anthony jokes. I give him a quick kick under the table. After the shocked expression fades, he breaks into a hearty laugh.

"He stalked me. Then he hired me to attend a fundraiser with him."

"What do you mean, he hired you?" David asks. He places a bite of meatloaf in his mouth and chews.

I look across the table at Anthony and see he's enjoying this. The merriment dancing in his eyes is unmistakable. I'll have to figure out a way to make him pay for my discomfort.

"I was an escort."

CHAPTER NINE

You could've heard a pin drop after my statement. I look around the table and see that both of his parents have stopped eating, and Anthony can barely contain his laughter.

I hear a slight cough coming from Claire, so I look in her direction. "Do you mean, like, a prostitute?" She says this calmly and without judgment. Her eyes are staring directly at me.

Anthony bursts into a full belly laugh while I'm left speechless. Claire's eyes move slowly to look at her son.

"No, Mom, she's not a prostitute. She attends social functions as a platonic companion. It's a great service to use when you need a date that doesn't expect dinner and flowers. I saw her at the Los Angeles Food and Wine Festival, and I knew I wanted to date her. We went to Damon's cancer research fundraiser together. I asked her out, but she said she wouldn't mix business with pleasure, so I fired her. I was no longer a client, and she was free of her conflict. The rest is history."

"That will be an interesting story to tell your kids," David says as he puts another forkful of meatloaf in his mouth. At the mention of kids, my eyes dart to Anthony, and he is still beside himself, laughing.

"I love interesting stories, but I have to say that this one tops them all for me," Claire comments. "How did you ever get started in that business, Emma? It's not your average career."

"It's a long story, but the short version is I lost my mother at a young age. I had an absentee father, and at eighteen, I had to support myself." I take a sip of wine and continue. "My mom always told me to make sure I could take care of myself. I remember her telling me not to let any man take away my options. I met a nice man at a coffee shop, and he needed a date for a holiday party—the rest is history. In hindsight, I was careless in going out with a stranger, especially since he was so much older than me." My eyes meet with Anthony's as I say the word "older."
"I was fortunate. He turned out to be a nice man who ended up being a lot of help to me. All of my clients have come from that initial meeting. I only escort people who are referred to me. I don't date people I escort."

"Are you still in the escort business?" Claire asks.

"No, I quit after the first date with your son. I work for Anthony in the marketing department of Anthony Haywood's."

"She does an amazing job in our marketing department. Now that Ahz has opened, things have slowed down. I'm afraid she may get bored and want to leave me." Anthony looks across the table at me.

"Since you brought it up. Kat says they will be hiring a public relations representative for Ahz, and I'm thinking about applying. I like working at Anthony Haywood's. However, fetching coffee and checking print ads isn't quite as fulfilling as I'd hoped it would be. It's not why I spent four years in college." I see Anthony is not happy with this information. He knew I was getting bored, or he wouldn't have mentioned that he was afraid I'd leave him.

"I think it's great you went to college, and you're chasing your dreams. In my day, women were breaking free of the traditional wife and mother roles. I was more of a traditionalist. I loved staying home and taking care of my boys—Anthony and David are my world." She smiles warmly at her husband and then at Anthony. "I would've entered the workforce as a secretary if Anthony didn't sneak in there." She looks at her son with pride.

"My mom was the same. She was a stay-at-home mom until she passed away."

"We're so sorry to hear you lost your mom at such an early age. Aren't we, David?" Claire asks. David stops eating his meatloaf long enough to nod his head.

"Oh... Emma," Anthony says. "We're going to the Los Angeles Food and Wine Festival in a couple of weeks. I kept meaning to tell you, but I always forgot. Will you go with me?"

I love the way he says we are going but then asks if I want to attend.

"Of course, I'll go. You're talking about food and wine, two of my favorite things. There's no way I'm missing it." They have the best food and wine available. Who would pass that up?

"How is Damon?" Claire asks as she cuts her meatloaf in small bites as she waits for one of us to answer.

"He's great. He just got back from Hawaii." Looking up, he winks at me. "He's engaged to marry Emma's former roommate, Katarina. No date's been set, but I don't see Damon waiting too long."

"Oh, my goodness, he's engaged? How exciting." Claire claps her hands together. "I can't wait until the day my son comes home and tells me he's engaged." She looks straight into Anthony's eyes. "You're not getting any younger, and neither is your father and me. We'd like some grandchildren someday."

Now it's my turn to bust into a full belly laugh. Anthony's mouth drops open in shock.

"On that note, I think it's time to clean up and get on the road.

Em, and I have work tomorrow." He stands, picks up a few dishes, and heads to the kitchen.

We help clean up the dinner mess and gather our things so we can leave. Claire bags up some cookies for us to eat later. She clips a few yellow roses and then wraps the stems in damp paper towels and foil.

"It was such a pleasure to have you for dinner, Emma. My boy is pretty crazy about you." She gives me a hug and a kiss on the cheek.

"Thank you for having me. I'm pretty crazy about your son." I look up into the face of the man that has stolen my heart. Our eyes connect for only a minute, but that's all I need to see that Anthony Haywood loves me.

We walk hand in hand down the walkway and enter the car for the short drive home.

"Are you thinking of changing jobs?" He puts the car into gear and hits the accelerator.

"Yes, I think it would be a good position for me. I love talking to people, and I think I'd make a good ambassador for Ahz. It would also give me more time to see Kat. I rarely see her, and I miss her." I look to my left and see the grim line of Anthony's mouth. He doesn't want to share me with anyone. "You're going to have to learn how to share," I tease.

"I'm an only child, Emma. I have never had to share." The tension in the car is palpable. Who would've thought that considering a transfer would cause such a kerfuffle?

"Well, you're thirty-four, and it's time you learn that you don't always get your way." He's pissing me off.

"Why are you being so bitchy? I want you to be with me. Is it so hard to be with me? Things have been going well."

"Yes, things are going well, but I will not give everything up for you. I said I'd move into your house. I gave up my job for you. I'm making a lot of sacrifices." My voice seems to get away from me. "I can't put all of my eggs in your basket, Anthony. Everything about my life is about you right now, and that scares the shit out of me. What happens if we have a fight and one of us says that's it?"

"We're fighting right now, Emma. You're sitting here, yelling at me. I'm not ready to throw in the towel, are you? If you are, then you're not the girl I thought you were."

As the tears pour from my eyes, we pull into the garage of his house. He throws the car into park and exits in a huff. I sit in the passenger seat and weep. *What the hell just happened?* We had a lot of fun at his parents' house, and at the mention of me applying for a transfer, the entire night turned to shit. I sit in the car alone for what seems like an eternity. I pull out my phone and text my friend.

Trouble in paradise. Can you meet for lunch tomorrow?

Yes, let's meet at the taco shop on Sunset Blvd. at noon. Will that work? Are you okay? Do you need me now?

That will be good. I'm okay and no, stay home. I'm heading to bed soon, anyway.

Hang in there. See you tomorrow. Love you.

Love you too!

As soon as I push send, the lights in the garage turn on, and I see Anthony standing by the door.

"Are you coming in or what?" he growls.

I open the door to the car and step out. Wiping the residual tears from my eyes, I breeze past him and head straight for the bedroom.

"Wait up, Em. Let's not do this. I'm sorry. I don't know why we had this fight. I love you, babe. Please don't be mad at me anymore."

"I love you, too, but if you squeeze a chick too hard, you'll crush it to death. You have to understand that I have been on my own since I was twelve. I spent a lot of time with Kat's family, but I spent more time by myself than anyone else. I'm not used to this. I love you, but I need time to be me as well."

"I don't know where all of this came from. You've been pulling away a bit lately, and I'm feeling insecure. I'm sorry. I didn't know I was suffocating you."

"I'm having a tough week. I'm sorry, too. I love you, and I'll try not to be so bitchy."

"I'm sorry about that, too. It looks like I'll be trading in some of those brownie points that I've collected." He gives me a timid smile.

"Let's just go to bed," I say as I tug him toward our room. All the tension seems to have disappeared, and we are back to ourselves. Our first fight, and we came out relatively unscathed.

"Make love to me, Em. I need to feel you in my arms now more than ever."

I fall into his embrace. I love the feel of being wrapped in his arms. The first heated kiss sets off a frenzy of activity. All the tension from the day is waiting to be released at this moment. We quickly remove each other's clothes and climb into bed.

"I was expecting punishment sex, but makeup sex is going to be even better," I pant as he sinks himself deep inside me.

"Oh, you're going to get punished, all right. I'm going to take you hard for making me feel old today. Then I'm going to make love to you because I love you so much that it almost hurts me. If you're still mad at me after that, then we'll have makeup sex. By tomorrow morning, I want our minor disagreement to be a long-lost memory."

"For the record, I'm not mad at you, but I'll pretend to be to get the makeup sex. I hear makeup sex is the best."

He pulls me into his arms and begins an evening full of punishment and pleasure. It's hours before we fall asleep.

CHAPTER TEN

I awake, lying in his arms. Snuggling up to him, I try to get as close as I can. I can't believe how many times we made love last night. The first time was brutal, but in the best way. He was punishing me for pulling away from him and for calling him old. His desperation to have me was in every thrust. He pounded my flesh as if he were trying to climb into my body. I could almost hear him yelling "mine" each time our hips met. We took, and we gave until our appetites were replete and we collapsed in exhaustion.

His arms fold around me; even in his sleep, he pulls me closer, making sure I don't get too far away from him. I scoot my bottom next to his body and relax in his embrace. I have no idea what time it is, but I'd do anything to stay like this for the entire day.

"I called in sick for both of us today." I hear him whisper. "I thought we both needed the extra sleep. Since all you do is fetch coffee, I figured they could live without you. I cannot."

I can feel his erection pressing against my butt cheeks. I groan as he presses it forward. I'd love to make love to him this morning, but I don't have it in me.

"Thanks, baby, I can use the extra sleep. Someone kept me up all night long." I can't control the yawn that escapes from my mouth.

"Someone kept me up all night long as well," he replies, pushing his hardness against my bottom again.

"I can't do it again this morning. I'm too sore. You showed me no mercy last night."

"What? My twenty-four-year-old smokin' hot girlfriend can't keep up with her much older boyfriend? I'm shocked and disappointed." His hand rubs my hip. It feels so nice when he caresses my body. I could almost rally myself for another round, but I'm so tired.

"You win. You're a very young man, and I should've never given you such a hard time." I pull his arm around me and place his hand over my breast. I love to sleep with him like this.

"I'll be the only one giving anyone a hard time in this house. I hope to be giving you a hard time for many years to come, babe."

"Put that thing away for now. I need my sleep. I have a lunch date with Kat today, and I don't want her to think you beat me when I can't walk in the door on my own accord."

"Kat just got engaged. I'm sure she didn't do very much walking in Hawaii. She'll understand," he teases.

"Go back to sleep and hold me, old man."

"Are you going there again? Haven't you learned your lesson? I'm going to let you rest for now, but you're going to have to pay for that *old* comment later."

"I'm counting on it," I say as I pull him closer to me and drift off to sleep.

"You're late," Kat says as I rush into Amigos at nearly ten past noon.

"I know. I'm sorry. I was up all night having makeup sex, and I got a late start." I fall into the booth, sitting across from Kat. "Did you order the guacamole yet?"

"Of course. How long have we been coming here for tacos? They see us coming and immediately scoop the green stuff into bowls. Are you working today, or are you off?"

"I'm off all day. What did you have in mind?" Kat flags down the server and orders us two big margaritas. "Okay, spill the beans."

"Everything is okay now. I think I was just being overly sensitive about my independence, and I upset him. He was very calm during the whole thing. It was me who did all the yelling and screaming."

"That doesn't sound like you. What's up?" The server delivers the chips, guacamole, and two massive margaritas.

"I don't know. I've been in a funk all week. Maybe it's because last week was a hard week for me." I exhale and take a sip of my drink. "I've never had to answer to anybody. I got pissed off when I told Anthony I wanted to apply for a job at Ahz, and he didn't react the way I'd expected. He likes having me around."

"Is he treating you well, Em? I mean, he's not violent or abusive or anything, right?"

"Oh, God no, he's amazing. I think it wasn't the time to have that talk. It was one week after the anniversary of my mom's death. We talked about her a lot lately, and that brought up a lot of different memories. One of the most vivid memories is of her telling me never to allow a man to limit my options."

"Do you think he's trying to limit your options? I don't know him that well, but I don't see him as that guy."

"No, you're right. I think he's used to getting what he wants, and he wants me to work where he is. I don't like my job there. Everyone treats me with kid gloves because they know I'm sleeping with the boss. I'm not having an authentic work experience at Haywood's."

"If you're not happy, find something else, Em. You're not the type of person to settle. You never have been, so why are you starting now?"

The waiter approaches to get our lunch order. We get the same thing every time; chicken tacos for me and carne asada ones for her.

"You're right, but here's the thing, I'm venturing into unfamiliar territory. I've never been in love before, and I don't know how things are supposed to work."

"Em, I really don't know what advice I can give you. I'm new to this whole love thing, too. I can only tell you that you have to decide for yourself how things will work for your relationship. What works for one won't work for all."

"I'm sure you're right. Things are back on track. We made it through our first disagreement. The makeup sex was amazing. I'm thinking about making him mad more often just so we can do that again." I fan myself as if I'm hot.

"That good, huh? I think Damon and I have had enough drama for a lifetime. I'm just going to enjoy the peace and tranquility we have right now."

"I can understand. Let me see that ring again. I didn't get to ogle it at dinner the other night." She places her left hand in front of me. "How do you lug that stone around all day long? It must weigh a ton," I tease.

"It is huge, isn't it?" She looks down at her ring and smiles. I can tell she is blissfully happy. "I get my cast off on Wednesday. Yay!"

"Finally. That will make lugging this around much easier. So, did he get down on one knee and all that?" I ask. "I want all the dirty details."

"Yes, he did the whole down on one knee thing, champagne, flowers, and beautiful music." She raises her hand for a high five. "Hawaii was wonderful. It was peaceful and relaxing. We spent a week focused completely on us. I'd highly recommend that."

"I have no idea how you guys figured it all out in four months, especially after having to overcome so many hurdles along the way."

"I guess it just came down to the fact that we both loved each other and knew there would be no one else for either of us."

"That's what scares me, Kat. I think Anthony is the one. Having said that, I don't have a relationship track record I can compare anything to."

"Why's it scary? You should be full of joy, knowing you feel the same way about each other. He loves you, Em. He called today and is having us set up a prom night at Ahz just for you."

"He didn't!"

"Yes, he did. He said that, for whatever reason, you missed your prom, and he wants to make sure you experience it. We scheduled it for next month. It's a great idea, and I think you are going to have a great time marketing it."

"Why would I be marketing it? That job belongs to Trevor, and you, for that matter." Her face breaks into a goofy grin.

"You didn't hear it from me, but I think they have transferred you to Ahz. I got a memo this morning. It said you were the new PR person. You will work out of my office until they set one up for you. That should take a day or two. He's listening to you, Em. He hears you. He loves you."

A tear falls from my eye and runs down my cheek. I swipe it off my face and take a long swig of my drink.

"I don't know why I'm crying. I've been a mess lately. I'm happy for you, Kat. I'm happy for me, too. Anthony is a wonderful man."

We eat our lunch and drink another margarita. By the time the check comes, we are both too tipsy to drive. I pull out my phone and text Anthony.

Hey, you sexy, young thing, your lush of a girlfriend has had too much to drink. Can you pick me up? Kat too?

Where are you? Damon and I are at Ahz. We'll both come and fetch our women.

We are at Amigos on Sunset Blvd. Thanks, baby, I owe you.

I intend to collect. See you in twenty. Love you, babe! <3

You made me a heart. How sweet. You must love me.
You have no idea. We're on our way.

"Damon and Anthony are on their way. We have time for another margarita before they get here." I order two more drinks and ask for the updated check.

CHAPTER ELEVEN

Just as I drain the last bit of margarita from my glass, our men approach. Anthony leans in to kiss me before he plops down beside me.

"Your white knights have come to the rescue," Damon says. "Are you girls ready to go?" His eyes are on Kat as he asks the question. The love he feels for her shows in everything from his soft touch to the look in his eyes.

"Yep," I say. "I have to take this man home and have my way with him. He's an expensive chauffeur and will want payment in flesh right away," I slur.

"Well, you heard the lady," Anthony says. "She wants me. What can I say?" he laughs. "See you soon, Damon. Katarina. I better get my girl home."

Anthony helps me out of the booth and guides me to his car. He walks me to the passenger seat, helps me in, and buckles me up.

"Thanks, Anthony. You're the best man I know." He stands and looks at me for a moment. "I love you," I tell him.

"I love you, too, my drunk little redheaded spitfire. Let's get you home. We can get your car tomorrow."

"I love this car. Have I ever told you that? It's such a hot car for the hot man who drives it." After he gets me situated, he plants a kiss on my lips, then runs around the car and jumps in the driver's seat.

"You think the driver is hot, huh?" He winks at me while he buckles his seat belt.

"Oh...yes...I don't think I've met a man that makes me feel the way you do. I've never been in love before, but I swear the minute I heard your voice on the phone, I fell in love with you." I turn in my seat to look at him. He takes one hand off the steering wheel and holds my hand. "Kat tells me we have to define our own rules. What works for one person doesn't work for everyone."

"It sounds like you and Kat had a good talk. I'm glad you could meet for lunch." He says while chuckling.

"What are you laughing about?"

"I'm not sure you and Kat can handle working together. If you have lunches like this all the time, no one will get any work done."

"We were celebrating. She is so freaking happy, Anthony. I'm so happy for them."

"Did she tell you we are transferring you to Ahz so you two can work together?" As soon as he says the word "transfer," I break into a fit of tears. Thank goodness we are pulling into the garage. He throws the car in park, unbuckles me, and awkwardly pulls me over the gearshift and into his lap.

"What's wrong, Em?" His hand goes directly to my cheek and pulls my head around so he can see my face.

The tears stream down my face. I try to talk but can only get a word or two out at a time. "I... thought I... would... be happy, but now... I won't... see you all day long." I bury my head in his chest and continue to cry.

I don't know how we got out of the car or how he carried me downstairs. It took him only minutes to undress me and put me in bed. The last thing I remember is him telling me he loved me and that everything would be okay.

I wake up a couple of hours later with a massive headache. Throwing on a robe, I walk upstairs in search of Anthony and an aspirin. As I near his office, I hear him on the phone. His voice sounds full of concern.

"Mom, I don't know what to do. She seemed so miserable this past week. I don't know how to help her. I love her so much, but maybe I'm not enough. This is all new territory for me." There is a pause in his conversation. I don't want to eavesdrop, so I step into the doorway to let him know I'm up. His head pops up, and he looks at me. His eyes find mine, and a smile emerges from his lips. He gestures for me to come to him. "Hey, Mom? Thanks for everything. Em just got up from her nap, so I'm going to hang up. I love you." He hangs up the phone and pulls me into his lap.

"How are you feeling?" he asks.

"I feel like I never want to have another drink again. I don't know why I thought three margaritas at lunch was a good idea, but we got to talking, and I kept ordering." Anthony transfers me from his lap to his desk. He pulls my tie loose and lets the robe fall open. His hands reach inside and gently stroke my sides. The minute he touches me, I feel my body respond. I let my head fall back as I inhale. "Mmm," escapes my lips. He rolls his chair forward and presses his lips to my stomach.

"You have bewitched me. I don't know what to do with you, and yet I can't think of ever living without you."

"You don't have to live without me. I'm yours. Remember that movie that said something like, 'You had me when you said hello'?" I run my hands through his hair. "Well, you had me the minute I picked up the phone." I lean down to kiss him and feel my head throb from the motion. "I have a headache, and I'm told that sex is good for pain."

"Say no more. I aim to please." He picks me up and carries me not downstairs, as I would expect, but down to the beach. As the sun sinks into the blue ocean, the sky ignites with color. Flames of orange and red shoot out of the water, lighting up the sky as if the water was on fire. He sets me on my feet and disrobes me. Once he places my white robe on the sand, he gently lays me down on top of it.

"This is what we should have been doing yesterday. I believe I was lying just over there, panting your name," I say, remembering how I felt under his body then.

"I think in about two minutes, you will be panting over here, yelling my name."

Just the mental picture of what he is painting makes me moan with need. His clothes drop around him, and he stands naked in front of me. He kneels between my legs and peppers my face with soft kisses. I pull my hair back and out of the way to expose my neck. I love it when he kisses my neck. He understands without words and runs his tongue from the base of my neck to my ear. I feel him pull my earlobe into his mouth and bite gently. His tongue runs along my jaw to my chin and delivers him back to my mouth, where he kisses me deeply.

I feel his hardness against me. It needs no guide to know how to get home. He nudges at the edge of my sex and retreats. Each push penetrates a little deeper. Every time he pulls back, his penis grabs my moisture. With the roll of his hips, the velvet head of his shaft glides across my wet folds and massages me. He knows how much that drives me crazy. My body quivers with need as he teases me.

His arms are shaking with the strain of keeping his body elevated over mine. Tired of waiting for him, I grab him by the ass and pull him hard into me. He gasps as his body collapses on top of mine. I feel the weight of him crushing me into the soft sand beneath my robe. He moves in a steady rhythm as he loves me completely. Every move of his body is a silent message. Every thrust screams the words, *I love you*.

I can feel his body tense. I love that feeling just before he releases when everything is on fire, and every cell is awake. He shifts slightly so the friction is centered perfectly. I feel the ground fall away as my orgasm glides over the edge. I dig my nails into his shoulders, trying to hold on to something solid while I fall through space. I look into his eyes as he loses himself in me. Feeling the pulse of his climax as his hot release coats me. He calls out my name, and my heart twists at the amount of love I feel for this man.

We lie in each other's arms as the sun completely disappears and the stars twinkle. I think this may be my favorite moment so far.

"Take me into the water," I tell him as I try to stand on wobbly legs.

"You don't like the ocean."

"No, but I love a man who loves the ocean. And I will learn to love what he loves. Take me to the water, but don't let me down."

He picks me up and carries me into the water. I feel safe in his arms as the coolness laps against our bodies. I hold him tight, making it seem like we are connected. After tonight, my heart is fused to his forever.

CHAPTER TWELVE

The smell of fresh coffee wakes me from a sound sleep. The dip of the bed tells me I'm not alone. I curl in the direction the bed is leaning and find myself nudged up against the thigh of a very handsome man. His prickly hair tickles my cheek as I kiss his leg. His hand comes up to massage my shoulders.

"Oh, that feels so good. My body aches today. Will you rub my lower back?" I ask.

"Roll over, and I'd be happy to give you a quick back rub. Then we have to go to work. I brought you coffee, and there is oatmeal waiting upstairs for you."

"Okay, let me run to the potty first. I'll be right back." I jump out of bed and dash to the bathroom to empty my bladder. As soon as I wipe, I laugh.

"What's so funny in there?" he asks from the bedroom.

I finish what I need to do and stroll back into the bedroom with a smile on my face. "I know why I've been so moody lately. I just started my period. No wonder I've been up and down. I'm so sorry, baby. I must have put you through hell."

"Thank God! I was thinking that maybe I wasn't making you happy."

"You make me very happy. I love you. Never think that, okay?"

"I noticed you don't have a regular cycle. Why is that?" His eyes look to me in question.

"I take the mini-pill. It's been good so far, but my periods are always sporadic. I wonder if being as sexually active as we are influences my cycle? I'll have to visit my doctor and see if she can recommend something more predictable. It would be nice to know when I'm going to get a visit from Mother Nature; that way, I can prepare you for my onslaught of irrational emotions."

"Lie down so I can rub your back. It's probably cramps."

I lie down on my stomach and relax under his firm hands. He kneads my lower back like a baker kneading bread. "I'm not sure if I'm happy that you know so much about women or if it should upset me you have had so many before me."

"You should be happy I have learned enough to apply the good stuff to you and know that after you—there will be no others."

"You say the sweetest things. I don't know how to respond."

"You don't get it yet, do you? I knew from the moment that I saw you across the room that you were it. I can't explain it; I just knew. When I asked you to move in with me, it wasn't so I could shack up with you. I want you here with me because my life is better when you're around. I feel at peace. I don't feel like I have to keep proving myself to others. All I want is to prove myself worthy of you."

I turn around and look up at the man baring his soul to me. "You have nothing to prove to me. I'm just a poor girl from Arcadia who fell in love with a poor boy from Hollywood."

"This poor boy can now buy you the moon if you wanted it."

"I love that he would buy me the moon, but I don't want the moon." My hands intertwine with his as he lifts them over my head and leans in to kiss me.

"I love that you don't need the moon to be happy." He gently kisses me, sucking my lower lip into his mouth. As he coaxes my lips open, I let out a little moan, leaving him the room he needs to explore me with his tongue. If he could have dumped all of his emotions into a kiss, it couldn't have been more potent than the one we are sharing right now. He breaks the kiss and leaves me breathless. "Get dressed and come upstairs. You need to decide where you're going to work."

I take the last bite of oatmeal and grab my purse before heading out to the car and jumping into the passenger seat.

"I'll take you to your car. Let's meet in my office when you get to work so we can talk about your new project."

"I remember something about prom being discussed before I became three sheets to the wind."

"Damn it. She wasn't supposed to tell you. But I suppose after three margaritas, she couldn't have kept anything to herself. Okay, well, let's talk about it when you get to the office."

We pull into the parking garage where I left my Audi yesterday. He waits for me to get in and buckle up before he goes. I follow him out and straight to the Anthony Haywood headquarters.

Being here always makes me feel like a naughty employee. I see everyone's eyes when we walk into the building together. Some look like they're asking themselves if I'm just the flavor of the month, while others look at me with envy. I know how they feel; if I had to watch him with another woman, I'd come undone.

The fact that he's mine still shocks me. What do I know about love and relationships? I have no idea what a healthy one should look like. I know what we are doing is working for me. I have to stop freaking out about how we got this close this fast.

"Come on in and close the door." He takes a seat in the big chair behind his desk. I sit in a chair in front of his desk. "So, you heard I want to do a prom night promotion. When I heard you didn't attend your prom, I wondered how many people didn't get to attend their prom, and it made me think about how successful a do-over could be." He leans back and puts his shoes on the desk. "To have you spend more time with Kat and utilize your marketing skills, I thought you could be in charge of marketing this idea. I talked it over with Damon, and he thinks it's a great plan. You will be taking on the PR position, but since that's not a full-time job right now, we gave you something else to keep you busy."

"You want to throw an adult do-over prom so that I can experience it? Are you crazy?"

"Yes, I think I may be. Why is it you didn't attend your prom?"

"I was working. I had a job that night, and I needed the money more than I needed to go to prom. You have to remember I was getting evicted from my house. My aunt told me I was getting the boot at eighteen. I could've stayed with Kat, but it was time to start my own life."

"It pisses me off that your dad was so callous toward his daughter. I have the investigator looking into things, but so far, he hasn't turned up anything. Why didn't your grandparents step in to help?"

"I never met them. My dad's parents were deceased, and my mom's parents were absent. The aunt that stayed during the week was my dad's sister. She got paid to stay with me. You have no idea how lucky you are to have your parents."

"I know how lucky I am. By the way, my mom loves you. She thought you were stunningly beautiful and can't stop talking about how cute her grandchildren are going to be," he says with a roll of his eyes.

I burst into laughter. "Did you know the first thing she told me was that in her day, you didn't get to 'try it before you buy it'?" I give him a goofy look and watch his eyes bulge.

"Did she really? That is too freaking funny. Almost as funny as when she asked if you were a prostitute."

"Yes, that was a real charming moment. Why is it you threw me to the wolves at your parents' house?"

"I knew they would love you if I loved you. I loved the way you interacted with them. I found it humorous to throw you and my parents off-kilter at the same time." Lowering his feet, he leans across the table and holds my hands. "I knew my mom liked you when she cut her prized roses and gave them to you."

"Her Julia Child rose if I remember correctly." I can't stop shaking my head. He thinks he's a real comedian.

"She planted that rose bush the day I opened my first restaurant. That was ten years ago."

"She is very proud of you, and rightly so. You would be everyone's fantasy son."

"Yeah, well, I wasn't as good as everyone makes me out to be, but I turned out okay. I can pay my bills, and I'm not living in her basement at thirty-four."

"I could only hope to have children as unruly, unmotivated, and uninspired as you." I roll my eyes. "Enough about our virtual children. Tell me about this prom night."

"It's your night, baby, so make it what you want. Let Damon and me know what your fantasy prom night would include, and we'll try to make it happen. We can't change the band because those schedules are set well in advance, but whatever else you want is fine."

"How long do I have to plan and promote this night?"

"Not long. We are squeezing it in next month."

"Perfect. Now I have to find a dress and a date in less than a month." I knew he would react if I said I had to find a date.

"Emma Lloyd, will you accompany me to prom?" He is still holding my hands and grinning at me like a sixteen-year-old boy.

"I'll think about it. Can I give you my answer tomorrow? I'm holding out for that one special boy."

It doesn't take him but a second to round the desk and pull me into his arms. "You're holding out for the highest bidder, huh? What do I have to do to get you to say yes?"

"You'll have to get your Chucks to match my dress," I tease.

"Done. Now get to work, or I'll dock your pay for slacking off in the boss's office."

"I don't even know where I work anymore. You had me transferred." After yesterday, I'm a bit confused.

"You are free to work wherever you want. You said you missed Kat, so I thought you wanted to work at Ahz. Where do you want to work? I can set you up a desk here if you want to share my office. You can have your own office, or you can work at Ahz. The world is your oyster, babe."

"Wow, sleeping with the boss has its perks, doesn't it?" I push my lips into his and wiggle my body into him.

"Don't start something you can't finish, Emma," he warns. I can feel his arousal twitch against my stomach.

"Office sex; I've never done it, but Kat tells me it's amazing. We'll have to try it once my monthly friend leaves." I push away from him and dash to his door. "See you tonight, baby. I'm going to work at Ahz today."

I find Kat in the VIP lounge. Her head is bent over a notebook. Her cell is glued to her ear, and she is having a very animated conversation. She sees me walk in and waves me over. I point to her soda to see where she got it, and she points toward the bar. When you know someone as well as we know each other, no words are needed.

"Okay, so lemon drops and chocolate-covered bacon. Is there anything else?" There is silence on Kat's end, but I can hear the soft sound of a voice on the other. "No, sorry, I can't obtain anything that would send me to jail. I look forward to meeting the band. See you Friday." Kat hangs up the phone and exhales. "You'd think I was a pimp or a dealer with the requests I get. I can get chocolate-covered bacon, but I draw the line at prostitutes and cocaine."

"Well, I could probably help you out with the prostitutes since Anthony's mom thinks I used to be one."

"How did we get so lucky to meet two wonderful men on the same night?" She looks down at her hope diamond and smiles. "Are you going to withhold sex from him because he did you wrong? I would. I'd make him pay hard for making you squirm at his parents' house. It's hard enough to meet the mom, but for him to set you up. I'm thinking a month, and a good case of blue balls should guarantee that doesn't go down again."

"Look at you, all hard ass and shit. What happened to my sweet little Kat?" I poke her in her side, knowing how ticklish she is.

"I met Damon Noble," she says, giggling.

"Okay, enough said. So, what are we going to do about this prom idea?"

"We? This is all you, my dear. I have a job, but I'm going to attend because my first prom date was boring. I can guarantee I will get lucky after this soiree; Damon is a sure thing."

"Just don't do any of your exhibition shit at my prom," I warn her.

Bringing her phone to her ear, she sticks her tongue out at me. While Kat makes her call, I pick up my phone and text Chris.

Hey, my brother from another mother. I still haven't heard from your girl.

Nice to hear from you, sis. Trevor and I are hitting Trax tonight. They have a Mad Monday promo with two-for-one martinis. She should be there. I'll let her know, and I'll put a fire under her ass to call you.

Thanks. I need to get someone in the house. It's more about security than money. All she needs to pay for is the gardener and the utilities. It's not a bad deal when you think about it. I'm never there, so it's like having your own house for next to nothing. You can tell her my last roommate met a millionaire while living there.

I'll tell her the owner is banging a billionaire. Maybe that will sway her.

Screw you...

Nah... never liked the vag. Love you, girl.

Yeah, Yeah. Give Trevor my love. Oh, I'm in charge of setting up an adult prom night at Ahz for next month. I'd love any ideas you have.

Ooh, I may get to wear satin after all. Trevor and I are in.

Talk to you later.

I get a Diet Coke from the bar and take a walk around Ahz. If I choose the venue first, maybe I can begin to feel the theme. I know for sure that the "prom" won't be held in the VIP lounge or on the sixth floor. There is no way I am having people peek up at my goodies from the floor below. I decide to have the main event on the third floor, where they play the eighties and nineties music primarily. I love the music from those decades, and I know Anthony will enjoy it, too.

Now that I have a venue and a musical direction, I have to decide on the theme. I go over the typical themes like casino, roaring twenties, under the stars, but I'm feeling in love right now. I decide to work with the letters in prom and come up with a message to Anthony. With my direction set, I contact the marketing department and make the arrangements.

I find my way down to Kat's office and sit behind her desk. Looking forward, I see Trevor through the windows. His desk sits directly across the hallway from Kat's. He looks up from his paperwork and smiles at me. I point to myself, and then I point back to Trevor; it's my silent way of asking if I can come over for a visit. He shakes his head yes. I slide out of Kat's chair and head on over.

"Hey, chickadee, I hear you're a permanent fixture over here. Did you tire of your hunk of burnin' love over there at Haywood's?"

"No, I just got tired of fetching coffee for the marketing director. While we were opening Ahz, I worked for Anthony, and that was great. Since then, things have taken on a much slower pace, and I have to stay busy. You know what they say about idle hands."

"No, what do they say about idle hands?" he asks.

"I don't have the foggiest, but I'm sure someone has said something." I laugh at myself. "I need some catalogs where I can find decorations for prom. Do you have any you would recommend?"

Trevor is up and out of his seat before I can finish my sentence. He walks over to a tall cabinet in his office corner and takes out a pile of catalogs.

"Here are a few. If you don't find what you're looking for, then let me know. I have about a hundred more. What is the theme?"

"I don't know that I have an actual theme, but I'm going for a 'love is in the air' kind of atmosphere. I look around me at all of us and see the love connection, and I want to play off that. I need the third floor reserved for the event. Who do I see about that?"

"I'll take care of it. It would be me you see about that, anyway. I'm glad you're here." He walks around and hugs me. "Katarina and I reserve the second Friday for lunch and shopping. We make an afternoon of it. You should join us."

"I'd love that. I need a dress for the food and wine festival. You can be my fashion consultant."

"I'm your girl," he says as his smile goes big and bright.

CHAPTER THIRTEEN

The last two weeks have passed in a flash. I can't believe how perfect the new job has been for me. I am the voice of Ahz. I have done a few press conferences for upcoming events. I'm organizing commercials and print ads to showcase the booked bands, and I've been working incredibly hard to pull off a short-notice prom. Although Anthony wanted *me* to have a prom, I can only think of him as I'm choosing everything.

Tomorrow's the Los Angeles Food and Wine Festival, but today is lunch and shopping with the girls. Well, Trevor and Kat—close enough. We agree to meet out front at noon. I'm the first to show up. While I'm waiting, I pull out my phone and text Anthony.

Hey, just getting ready to head out to lunch and go shopping. I'm buying a dress for tomorrow. Do you have requests?

Hmm, if we were alone, I'd say no dress needed. Since we'll be amongst thousands of my closest friends, I think a nun's habit might be best. Stay away from the margaritas.

No drinks for me today. I don't think there's a big demand for a habit, but I'll see what I can come up with. I love you and miss you.

I love you, too. See you tonight, baby.

I put my phone in my pocket and look up just in time to see Trevor and Kat approach.

"Let's have sushi for lunch," Trevor says as he bounces down the sidewalk toward me.

"I'm good with whatever," Kat and I say at the same time. We look at each other and laugh.

"You guys are like twins separated before conception. Let's go. We have to eat before you girls kill me with a marathon day of shopping. I'm thinking something like the *Pretty Woman* dress at the polo match," Trevor says as he looks at me. I know he's referring to the chic brown polka dot dress that Julia Roberts wore in the movie.

"I don't think I can pull off the *Pretty Woman* look, although I like the idea of a light summer dress. We'll hold the event inside, but there will be thousands of people. I imagine it will be hot and stuffy. What are you wearing, Kat?"

"I have no idea. I hope to find a cute skirt and blouse today."

We stop at Roko Sushi, where we grab a quick lunch before heading to Nordstrom. If you can't find it at Nordy's, you won't be able to find it anywhere. Trevor goes right to work, setting up dressing rooms for both of us. Like a personal shopper, he runs through the racks as if he works in the store. He chooses several things for us, then directs us to our respective dressing rooms before sitting in a chair as if he were Rachel Zoe. If he weren't such a fabulous marketing manager, he could make a go as a fashion consultant.

I step out in the first dress he chose for me. It's a red shift dress. I barely get out of the dressing room before Trevor frowns and sends me back to change. This dress looks like a paper sack.

I try the green one next. It's adorable with a fifty's flair to it. It's a Basque cut with a cinched waist and full skirt, and the bodice is a conservative scoop neck. It's not a habit, but it's sexy in a traditional way. I step into the nude heels and make my way out of the dressing room to see the critic. As soon as I emerge, I watch Trevor sit up straight and smile. He rises to his feet and heads toward me. With his hands on his hips, he walks a complete circle around, checking me from every angle. If I didn't know he was a gay man, I'd have been uncomfortable under his gaze.

"Oh, Em, it's the perfect dress. I love everything about it." Kat stands in front of me, wearing the cutest little pleated, ice-blue skirt and sweater set. It's adorable and fits her personality perfectly. It's short and sexy but sweet and innocent at the same time.

"I love what you're wearing as well. I think that would be perfect. It's such a great color for you," I say.

Trevor is standing back with the look of a proud parent on his face. He leans against the wall, arms crossed in front of his chest as if he's saying, "I told you so."

"Okay, ladies, get changed. We need to accessorize."

Trevor is an accessory diva. That poor man was born in the wrong body and would've made an excellent girl.

We head to the costume jewelry department and try on just about every piece of jewelry available before deciding on the pieces we like. Trevor says that jewelry is like the icing on the cake. You don't buy a cake because it's a cake; you buy it because it looks good.

"Has Roxy called you yet?" Trevor asks. He holds a pair of enormous gold hoop earrings beside my ears.

"Those are entirely too big," I say.

"You know what they say: the bigger the O, the bigger the ho." He puts the enormous hoops back on the rack. "So has she called or not?"

"Yes. She called me during the week, and we had a pleasant chat. I'm meeting her at the house on Sunday. So far, she seems cool."

"I think you'll like her. She's not like anyone I've ever met before," he says.

"I'm looking forward to it. I need to get someone in the house. It's not good to have your house empty for too long. I worry about someone breaking in because they think it's vacant. It's a decent neighborhood, but it's not Bel-Air."

"Let me know how it goes. Chris and my reputation are on the line if you don't like her."

"I'm still not happy about being replaced," Kat pipes in, "but you're right about leaving the house vacant. I'll get over there soon to finish cleaning out my closet."

"No worries, there isn't much left in there," I tell her.

With our arms full of bags and our wallets a little lighter, we make the walk back to Ahz.

"I can't believe the dress was three hundred dollars. That was insane, but it's so perfect." I say as we round the corner to Ahz.

"You have a billionaire boyfriend; make him pay for it," Trevor says.

"We don't have that kind of relationship. I've never asked him to pay for anything. He has a ton of money, but he lives a simple life. I make enough to buy my stuff," I reply.

"Girl, what's the point of having all that money if you can't enjoy it?" Trevor looks at me as if I've grown another head.

"Oh, he enjoys it. I don't think he wants for anything. As for me, I've always taken care of myself. I've had some help along the way, but mostly, I try to depend on myself."

"Speak of the devil," Kat says. I follow her eyes and see my hunk of burnin' love walking out the door of the restaurant at Ahz. He doesn't look pleased.

"See you later," I say as I make a mad dash to Anthony. He sees me coming and throws out his arms to hug me. I drop my bags just before I reach him and jump into his arms, wrapping my legs around his waist. Looking over my shoulder, I see my friends disappear into the employee entrance of the building.

"Wow. That was quite a greeting. Did you miss me?" he asks with little enthusiasm. He seems troubled by something.

"Yes, I missed you so much. What are you doing here?" I slide down his body and set my feet firmly on the ground. He reaches down and grabs my bags.

"There's a problem Damon, and I have to address. Since you're going to get some calls about it, I figured I'd wait for you so we can all come up with a plan together. Let's go. Damon is waiting for us in the conference room." Well, that doesn't sound good. I follow him back to the conference room located behind the restaurant. There are a few offices back here, but most of the offices are at either Anthony Haywood's Corporate Offices or Zenith.

Anthony leads me into the conference room and sets my bags by the door, then guides me to a seat near the head of the table. Damon is already there. He finishes up on the phone call he is currently engaged in.

"I have asked Katarina to come in. Since she will be my wife, this situation is going to affect her as well."

I look at the expressions on both men's faces. Upon closer inspection, Anthony looks tired, while Damon's expression is one of intensity.

"What's going on? You both look like someone just stole your favorite toy."

The door opens to the conference room. Kat walks in and takes a seat next to Damon. "What's up? Your text is concerning."

I'm the only one that has no clue what's going on. "Would someone tell me what's happening?" I demand.

CHAPTER FOURTEEN

Anthony clears his voice before he speaks. "I got a call from a *Los Angeles Times* reporter about two hours ago. He was calling as a courtesy. Last night, a drunk driver plowed into a crowd near the Nokia Center. When the person was arrested, they had an under twenty-one stamp on their hand from Ahz. Unfortunately, their blood alcohol level was at .21. We have pulled all the security footage and have a team looking through it with a fine-toothed comb. I promised the reporter an exclusive look into Ahz if he would hold on to the story until tomorrow. He'll call you, Emma, to set up a time to come and meet you."

I am shocked by this information. There is no way anyone under twenty-one got a drink at one of our bars. We have a nearly foolproof policy in place. "The first thing we need to do is prepare a statement." I look around the table at everyone. "My suggestion would be just to say we're investigating the allegations," I offer. "Will we lose our liquor license in the interim?"

Damon runs his hands through his hair and exhales. "No, the only way we will lose our license is if they can prove we served an underage drinker. This is an awful situation to be in, and I can't say how important it is that we don't give out too much information until we know the facts."

"Damon's right; the security footage will tell the story. The report will be ready for us tonight. The fact that Damon and I are owners will increase the media attention. Not to sound arrogant, but we are worth a ton of money, and there are many people who'd be happy to see us fail."

"Are you sure you want me to handle this for you? I'm new at this job, and I don't want to mess it up." I pinch the bridge of my nose. I can feel the stress that this is going to weigh on all of us. If Ahz goes under, then Kat, me, and hundreds of other employees will be looking for a job, not to mention the financial and emotional impact it will have on Damon and Anthony.

"I've known Emma for over a decade, and I think she is the perfect representative. She is quick on her feet and speaks with intelligence and eloquence." Kat leans back in her chair but keeps her eyes on Damon.

"I agree with Damon. Let's keep it to a brief statement if they ask us. Once the investigation finishes, we can figure out if we need to address it in a more in-depth manner," Anthony says.

A cell phone rings, and we all check our phones instinctively. Anthony answers his and walks toward the door to talk privately. Within a few minutes, he's off and returning to the conversation. "Sorry, that's something else I've got going on. My plate seems to be pretty full right now. You all know I'll be heading to Texas on Sunday. I should be back by Wednesday."

"We got this. Go find out what's happening in Texas, and we'll hold down the fort here," Kat says.

"All right, then. Let's talk tomorrow at the festival. I don't see anything else happening tonight." Damon helps Kat up, and they walk hand in hand out of the door.

"Are you okay?" I ask Anthony. I walk over to him, take his hand in mine, and look into his eyes. I'm a staunch believer the eyes are the windows to the soul. The eyes will always tell you the entire story. His eyes look tired and almost beat today.

"Yeah, I'm just tired. Let's go home. Let's relax in front of the television." He goes to retrieve my bags over by the wall.

"I can get those." I reach to take the bags, but he pulls them out of my way.

"I'll grab these," he says as he places all the bags in one hand. "Do you mind grabbing something for us to eat on the way home? I have to make a few phone calls. I'll meet you at home." He leans over and kisses me. It's not a passionate kiss, but one you give out of habit.

We walk to the garage together and enter our cars. As we exit, he turns right, and I turn left. This is the first time I've noticed Anthony and I going in different directions.

I PULL into the garage and park next to Anthony's Vanquish. My car smells of baked chicken, Cajun rice, garlic butter greens, biscuits, and the peach cobbler I brought for dessert. I balance all the containers and make it into the kitchen without dropping anything.

The house is quiet, and everything is closed up. Usually, Anthony walks into the house and throws the doors to the deck wide open. I walk over and open the doors myself, then go to work plating up our dinner.

Once the food is ready, I search for Anthony and find him in his office. His back is turned to me, but I can hear one side of the conversation he's having with the person on the other end.

"Okay, so they forced her, is what you're telling me. What else have you found out? Uh-huh. Okay. We can go over it in depth next week. Certainly. Goodbye."

I make some noise, so he knows I'm entering his office. He

swivels his chair around and looks in my direction. It's nice to see he still has a smile for me.

"I have dinner ready. I went to the Cajun place and picked up chicken and rice. Do you want to join me on the deck?"

He reaches out and grabs me around the waist, pulling me to stand between his legs. He buries his face into my stomach and lets out a groan.

"What can I do to help? It sounds like you've had an awful day."

"It's been okay. I have a lot of things going on at once. I feel like my hair is on fire. How was your day?" He leans back and looks up into my eyes.

"Good. While I was playing hooky from work, your day was going to shit, but hey, I have a magnificent dress for tomorrow," I tease. "But I'm sorry I wasn't there for you."

"Emma, you have nothing to be sorry for."

"All right, but you don't have to carry the weight of this on your own. Let's eat and then watch a *Lethal Weapon* marathon." I tug him up from his seat and push him into the kitchen. We take our plates and walk out onto the deck. The ocean has a way of calming his nerves. We sit in relative silence and eat our food. My thoughts are running amok, with most of my attention on the current Ahz crisis. I keep playing plausible scenarios in my head, but nowhere can I come up with one in which they served a minor alcohol.

"Do you think that having an 'eighteen and over' night is a good idea? I'm just wondering if you and Damon should reconsider your position on that." I take a bite of chicken and wait for his reply.

"We might have to rethink that. We wanted to have an all-inclusive club. The eighteen to twenty crowds are our regulars for tomorrow. If we reel them in now, we won't have to target them later." He takes in a deep breath and looks out over the water. "It was a great marketing idea; however, who would've thought a drunk driver with a stamp from our club would plow through a crowd of bystanders? I just found out that they've upgraded the one person in critical condition to stable, which is fantastic news."

"That's excellent news. Was that who you were talking to when I came into your office?" I gather both of our plates and stack them in front of me.

"No, that was the investigator from Texas. He was getting back to me on his findings. Your mom was forced to marry your dad after getting caught in a compromising position. He has a lead on someone who was friends with your mom and plans to meet with them tomorrow or Monday." He wipes his mouth with a napkin. "And I plan to meet with him while I'm in Dallas." "I appreciate your dedication to uncovering my past. It's turning out to be exactly as we thought. She was pregnant and had to marry him. I feel so sad for my parents. If they had to marry each other because of an unwanted pregnancy, I could understand why they wouldn't have a loving marriage. That in no way justifies the violence, but I can understand the frustration. No one should have to marry because of that."

"I'm so sorry, baby. I wish I could change it for you."

I shrug. I wish I could change it too, but that's a wish that will never come true. What's done is done.

Finished with our dinner, we both enter the house. I take the dishes to the sink to rinse them and place them in the dishwasher. Anthony gets the TV ready for our Mel Gibson marathon. I curl up next to him, and we both relax. I must have fallen asleep because the last thing I remember was watching the scene where the house on stilts gets pulled off its foundation by Riggs.

CHAPTER FIFTEEN

The churning in my belly sends me racing to the bathroom. I barely make it to the toilet before I spill the contents of my stomach. The spicy foods from yesterday come back up with a vengeance. My esophagus and stomach are on fire. I lie on the cool tile floor, in my T-shirt and underwear, waiting for the nausea to subside.

"Are you okay?" Anthony asks from behind me. "Let me get you a damp washcloth."

All I can do is groan. I feel like a train wreck. I sit up and lean against the wall. In the next second, I'm back praying to the porcelain gods. With nothing left in my stomach, the dry heaves take over.

Anthony pulls my hair back into a rubber band. These are the days I'm happy that so many women came before me. He places the damp cloth against my forehead and carries me back to bed.

"You're pale and clammy feeling. Let me get the trash can in case you feel sick again and can't make it to the bathroom. I'll call Katarina and Damon and tell them we won't be going to the festival today."

"No, let's wait. I ate that sushi yesterday, and then the spicy food last night. I think my stomach probably couldn't handle both. This used to happen when I was a kid. If I ate too much spicy stuff, I'd get sick. Wasabi is not my friend."

Anthony gives me a wary look. "Okay, but if you're not completely back to normal by noon, we aren't going." According to Anthony's tone, there will be no discussing the matter.

"Don't be silly. Even if I can't go, you should. There are so many people who want to see you and hear about the new club." I try to lift my head to look at him.

"We'll talk about it later. Try to go back to sleep. I'm going to make you some mint tea and dry toast."

I wake up several hours later next to Anthony. He has his laptop on his legs and is deeply concentrating on something. I roll over and snuggle next to his hip.

"Good morning. How are you feeling?" He brushes the loose strands of my hair away from my face.

"Better. I'm dehydrated, but I feel fine. I feel terrific. It was definitely the spicy foods. What time is it?" I stretch like a cat, trying to erase the kinks from a morning spent in bed.

"I put some tea in the carafe by your side of the bed. I also brought down some saltines in case you needed them. We didn't have any bread for toast." He puts his laptop to the side and reaches over to pour me some tea.

"Thanks. You didn't need to stay here with me. You would have probably been more productive at your desk." I sit up and sip the tea. It's still piping hot, so I'm forced to blow on it to cool it down. "What are you looking at?"

"I got the report from security this morning, and there is no sign of anyone serving the young lady a drink in the club. In fact, she left Ahz at nine o'clock."

"That's excellent news. I had no idea it was a girl. So, will the issue just go away?" I ask hopefully.

"No, although the burden of proof is on the police department, we'll do our investigation. I have hired another private investigator to find out where she went after she left there. The parking garage video shows her walking out of Ahz, and she looks sober. I feel some relief at that, but the press is still going to eat us alive."

"I don't understand why they always go for the jugular. I suppose it's whatever gets them a headline," I sigh.

"I guess." Setting everything aside, he scoots down the bed and lays his head in my lap. I ran my fingers through his hair. "Are you sure you don't want to stay home?" he asks.

"No, I feel fine. I just need to take a shower to feel human again. Where are my bags from yesterday?" I haven't seen them since I left Ahz.

"I hung everything up in the closet. I love that dress. It's a great color for you." He lifts his head from my lap and sits up in bed.

Peeling myself away from him, I climb out of bed and walk to the closet. There it is, hanging just where he said it would be. He's such a considerate man.

"Do you want to shower with me?" I smile at him, giving him my best come-hither look. "You look like you could use some stress relief."

That is all it takes to get him moving. He is up and strips naked in seconds flat. The shower is being turned on, and our towels are already on the counter. Anthony is quick when he's properly motivated.

I slowly remove my T-shirt and underwear and climb into the shower with him. I wrap my arms around his waist and pull him close to me. His hands reach for the shower gel, and he begins his thorough cleansing of my body. He spends extra time on my girly parts.

By the time he reaches for the hand-held shower nozzle, I'm so weak in the knees I have to sit down. The tile of the built-in seat feels cold against my bottom and the swollen lips of my overheated center.

Looking forward, I'm eye to snake eye with Anthony. His erection bobs in front of me. I wrap my lips around his girth and draw him into my mouth. The sound of his gasp is all I need to motivate me. I now focus my complete attention on his pleasure. I ease him in and out slowly. I know the pace is torturous to him. The feel of my tongue as it slides along the opening of his head causes him to shudder. The shower nozzle falls from his hand and crashes to the floor. I grab the firm globes of his ass and pull him deep into my mouth in one mighty thrust. His quick intake of air coaxes me to continue. To suck him slowly but completely, making sure his length is in the warm folds of my mouth.

The water is running down my face as I pull away and look up to his eyes. They are dark with passion, hooded, and sleepy looking. Noticing quickly that the source of his pleasure has pulled away, he reaches down to grab the pulsing shower nozzle and places it between my aching thighs. The force of the stream makes me shudder as the pulse of the water beats against my swollen flesh. I spread my legs wider, opening myself to the pleasure he provides. I tense as my core tightens and my approaching orgasm crests.

Anthony pulls the stimulation away just before I peak. It seems to be our game. The anticipation is half the fun. The explosion of feeling once you do climax is the reward for waiting. He lifts me from the seat and sits in my place. With my back to him, he lowers me onto his length. The feeling of fullness sends bolts of electricity to my core. My insides are like molten lava. His hands guide my hips up and down in a slow, steady rhythm. His right hand slips around to my front to stimulate my swollen, achy sex. Arching my back, I fall against him as I cry out his name. I clench around his girth as my climax milks him with every thrust—his body tenses just before he moans in pleasure.

We sit in silence, trying to regain enough strength to finish our shower. After several minutes, I pick up the discarded shower nozzle and rinse. The still tender flesh quivers beneath the strong spray, forcing me to stand and hold on to the wall. I hang the showerhead back in its place and make quick work of washing Anthony. He leans naked against the tile wall while I scrub him from head to toe. No words are spoken, but I try to convey everything I feel with the touch of my hands and the song singing in my soul.

I SLIDE my feet into the flesh-colored pumps and stand upright. Anthony is finishing up by tying his emerald-green tie around his neck. I love the way he always tries to coordinate his clothes with whatever I'm wearing.

I walk over to him and ask for help with my new jewelry. He takes the chain and fastens the latch at the back of my neck. Pulling my hair out of the way, he kisses my neck and lets my hair fall down my back. Wrapping his hands around my waist, he pulls me against his chest. We stand in front of the mirror, looking at our reflection. Even in my shoes, he stands a few inches taller than me. I'm not a tiny woman, but his broad swimmer's shoulders dwarf me.

"You didn't get your swim in today." I turn toward him and straighten out the slight kink in his tie.

"I didn't want to leave you when you were feeling so poorly. I ended up taking part in a much more satisfying water sport later this morning." His brilliant white teeth show gradually as his luscious, full lips open in a broad grin. His smile is disarming. "I'm so glad you're feeling better. I thought maybe you had food poisoning. Food poisoning can be brutal and last for days."

"Nope, just a weak stomach. I'll have to be careful what I eat today and no alcohol for me. I'll be the designated driver if you'd like."

"And let you drive my beloved sports car? I gasp in horror at the thought," he teases. "I'll drive there, and you can drive home if I drink anything."

CHAPTER SIXTEEN

We enter the convention center and park in a spot reserved for Anthony. Walking to the front entrance is like walking the red carpet. They ask us to stop several times while they take our photos. Reporters seem to swarm everywhere. It strikes me as funny. If people knew how down-to-earth Anthony is, they'd probably lose interest. He doesn't live the jet-set lifestyle his income would lead people to believe he does. He's a simple man with simple needs.

The first thing that hits me as we walk in is the sheer number of smells I'm assaulted with. I say assault because the moment we enter, my senses are assailed by the pungent aroma of everything from curry to the sickly sweet smell of fresh-baked cookies. Any other day I'd have swooned at the scents coming from the various vendors, but today I'm overwhelmed.

Booths are set up everywhere, and each is showcasing some delectable morsel or beverage. People are strolling through the space as white-jacketed servers walk through the crowds, peddling whatever their trays are loaded with. I break free of Anthony's hand and head straight for the bar. A glass of sparkling water and a peppermint will remedy what ails me. I ask the bartender to put a splash of bitters in my drink. It's a surefire cure for a weak stomach.

"Still queasy, I see," he says as he orders his drink. I didn't realize he'd followed me over to the bar. I shouldn't be surprised; he always seems to know exactly where I am.

"I'm okay. It was just the first onslaught of smells, but now that I'm acclimating to it, I'm fine." He receives his Diet Coke and shakes his head.

"I knew we shouldn't have come. You look pale again." He narrows his eyes and purses his lips. He's not happy.

"I'm fine. I am," I respond, not sure if it's him or me I'm trying to convince.

He slips his hands into mine and threads our fingers together. We walk around the venue and mingle. I recognize the faces of Emeril Lagasse and Wolfgang Puck. As we round the corner, I hear the unmistakable voice of Paula Deen. I love her Southern twang. I feel the pull as Anthony directs me to a quiet corner where a younger man is sitting. He looks familiar, but I can't place his name. As we get closer, I realize it's Jamie Oliver. He has done so many positive things in addressing childhood obesity.

"Hey, Jamie, how are you?" I hear Anthony say. He walks over to the blond chef and shakes his hand.

"Anthony, so good to see you. I'm just hiding out here for a bit. The crowds can be overwhelming. Have a seat." He motions for us to join him at his table. "Who's this with you?"

I reach out my hand and offer it to the man in front of me. His warm hand embraces my own as he brings it to his mouth for a gentle kiss. If I weren't already in love with Anthony, I'd have swooned. "Hi, I'm Emma Lloyd." I pull my hand back down and place it in my lap.

"It's been a while since I've seen you, Jamie. This is my girlfriend—my Emma." Anthony pulls me possessively to his side.

"I've been in London for far too long," he says in his English accent.

"Watching you kiss my girl's hand, I think it's time you went straight back to your wife and kids in London, my friend," Anthony quips. I giggle at his comment.

After several minutes of chatting, we decide to make the rounds, leaving Jamie behind. I walk to where I see Kat and Damon standing near a wine vendor's booth.

"Love that outfit, Kat." I lean over and kiss her on the cheek. She turns around and smiles at me. She looks happy to be rescued from the endless drivel about this year's grape crop.

Kat and I head toward the corner of the booth, so we don't interrupt the conversation being held by Damon and the wine vendor. Anthony walks up to Damon and joins in their discussion.

"You look a little pale today. Are you okay?" Kat asks with concern in her eyes. "Are you sick?"

"I'm having a little tummy trouble today. Remember when I used to get sick from spicy foods?"

"It was the wasabi from yesterday, wasn't it? I was wondering why you ordered a spicy tuna roll. I thought it was brave, considering your history."

"It was so good, though. I felt fine until I walked into this room. I thought for sure I was going to throw up again. I was sick this morning, but I've grown accustomed to the smells, and I'm good now."

Kat and I talk for a few minutes until I feel a strange hand wrap around my waist. It's not Anthony's; I'd know his touch anywhere. I look to my left and see Blake Havers standing entirely too close to me. I think back to Anthony's description of him, and he does look like a slimy little worm.

He leans over and plants a wet kiss on my cheek that makes my skin crawl. I never had that reaction to him before. Maybe it's still my stomach bug. I reach down to his hand and try to break his grip on my waist, but he pulls me tighter against him.

"Hello, Mr. Havers, how are you? It's been a long time since I've seen you." I greet him with kindness, hoping he will just say hello and leave.

Kat gives me a look that says, *Who the hell is that?*

"Kat, this is Mr. Blake Havers. He is a highly esteemed food critic. Mr. Havers, this is my friend, Kat. She works at Ahz and is engaged to Damon Noble."

"It's a pleasure to meet you, Mr. Havers. Have you been to Ahz? Anthony Haywood's is there. You should come and dine with us someday. I'm sure Anthony and Emma would love to host you for an evening."

I subtly try to give Kat a dirty look that says, "no damn way." At the mention of his name, I see Anthony look our way. His smile fades to a grim line as he looks at Blake and his hand placement.

I try once again to pry his hand from my waist, but I'm unsuccessful in my endeavor to free myself.

Blake's face comes close to my face. He breathes against my ear and whispers, "You look all cozy, sidled up to Anthony Haywood. I watched you walk hand in hand around the venue today. Had I known that it was just a money thing, I'd have paid double to get into your pants." His tongue darts out and leaves a trail of his saliva down my neck. The smell of liquor on his breath makes my stomach lurch. It takes every ounce of energy to break free of his grasp and push him away from me. In his inebriated state, he stumbles back and crashes into a table, sending wine bottles and glasses flying everywhere.

Everything from that point on seems to happen in slow motion. Anthony sees me push Blake away from me and comes rushing to my aid. Kat grabs my arm and pulls me away from the chaos. Blake is covered in wine and broken glass. Several photographers are snapping pictures rapidly. How is it that there is always paparazzi around when you least need them to be? It's a photographer's dream, but a celebrity's nightmare.

Blake stands and brushes the glass from his trousers and turns on me once again. "You're just a whore for hire," he yells for the entire world to hear.

In the next instant, I watch as Anthony's right hand fists up and takes the shot. His aim is dead on. Blake Havers falls flat on his ass, out cold.

Kat pulls me farther off to the side and sits me down. She must have seen the shock in my face as the scene unraveled. I try to get up to see what's happening, but dozens of reporters are snapping pictures. This is going to be front-page news.

It doesn't take long for security to arrive. I'm grateful when they take all of us to a small room away from prying eyes and telephoto lenses. I just created a spectacle that will generate a lot of bad press for Ahz and Anthony.

I look over at him sitting in the corner. His expression is grim, and his eyes are full of fire. He's still pissed. The only thing keeping him under control is the paramedic looking at his hand. They seem to be checking to see if it's broken, and I watch for any sign that the injury is more serious than it is.

I see another paramedic running smelling salts under Blake's nose. He shoots up as if someone set his feet on fire. He looks disoriented, but as he sets his sight on me, it appears as if he has a good recollection of everything that has gone down.

I watch in horror as Blake asks to see a police officer. He is yelling that he wants to press charges. His face is mottled red as rage spews from his lips. "That whore's new John punched me." His hands flail around, pointing to me, and then to Anthony. "I will own you, Mr. Haywood. Everything you have will belong to me, including her. She is all about the money."

I'd have risen myself and rushed over to punch his face if I didn't see Anthony bolt for the man and land another direct hit. Blake Havers is silenced once again.

It takes two hours to sort through everything. The police fill out many reports, including one from me accusing Blake Havers of inappropriate sexual behavior. I could've accused him of kidnapping the minute he wouldn't let go of my waist and held me in place. His hands on my body can be categorized as sexual assault. They accuse Anthony of two counts of assault and battery.

In the end, we all drop the charges. It wouldn't suit any of us, or our careers, to be in court for years. That I could press serious charges against Blake left him no choice but to drop everything.

The paramedics wrap Anthony's hand in a bandage after stitching his right middle knuckle. It was the last blow that broke his skin. Kat has been by my side the entire time. Damon has been trying to calm Anthony down for the last half hour. The police escort us out of a back entrance so we can avoid the press. Unfortunately, they are waiting in the garage. I take Anthony's keys, and we dash straight for the Aston Martin. There is no way he can drive with his hand all bandaged up. We take a lifetime to maneuver our way into the car. We say nothing to the reporters except, "No comment."

I put the car in reverse and back out without hitting any cameramen. We spend the ride home in silence. I reach over and turn on the radio, only to hear the song "The Fighter" by the Gym Class Heroes playing. The irony is not lost on me. Anthony sits brooding in the passenger seat with his head leaning against the window.

"Do we need to listen to this song?" he asks.

I glance at him. I'm met with a look of fierceness that leaves chills running up my arms. I have never seen him look so angry.

"Change it to what you want. I didn't choose it; it's what was playing when I turned on the radio."

He reaches over and presses another button on the car stereo. The next song that plays is "Titanium" by David Guetta. It's as if the universe has created a playlist for our day.

I wind my way down the canyon and up the street we live on.

When I pull into the garage, I barely have enough time to put the car in park before he jumps out. We are still rolling forward when he rushes out and slams the door. I'm left alone in the garage again.

I turn off the ignition and sit for a few minutes in silence. I'm scared to go into the house. My heart races, and I feel a full-blown panic attack coming on. I haven't had one in years. My heart rate seems off, and I feel like I may die. I know I won't, but the feeling is awful. I can't breathe. There is an immense weight on my chest. My mouth is dry, and yet I'm sweating profusely. The scared feeling that overwhelms me is paralyzing.

There has been so much stress the last few days, and it's taking its toll on Anthony. The look on his face reminded me of my dad when my mom disappointed him. I understand he isn't my dad and isn't going to respond as my dad would, but it's hard not to go to that place.

What I want to do is run to Kat's house. It would've been my natural response to a crisis. However, I can't run away anymore, so I take a few deep breaths and inhale and exhale slowly. Once I get my breathing under control, I square my shoulders and exit the car. This situation isn't going away on its own.

I trudge into the quiet house and walk over to the sink to get a glass of water. I don't need to turn around to know Anthony's in the room, but as soon as I do, I see him looming over me. His expression is one of unadulterated anger.

"What the hell happened, Emma?"

I walk past him, not liking how he is trying to intimidate me. I've never seen this side of him. He's acting like a bully, and I did nothing to deserve his wrath.

"What do you mean, what happened? I didn't do anything except push Blake away. He was inappropriate, and he licked my damn face. I tried to get him to loosen his grip on me. He wouldn't let me go, so I had to push him hard. He was drunk, and he stumbled backward. He hit the table and sent everything crashing."

"Did you sleep with him?" he yells. I don't know if I'm more surprised by the question or the tone of his voice. It's not a question. He thinks I slept with Blake.

I can't even think at this point. My world is crumbling around me. I knew things were going too well for too long. I stare at Anthony for a second and turn to walk away.

"Don't you walk away from me," he yells louder. "You can't run from this, Emma. The man publicly called you a whore. I have to ask myself why a man would do that?"

The tears are stinging my eyes as they pour down my cheeks. "If you have to ask that question, then you don't know me. I thought you were coming to defend my honor today, but you were just worried about your reputation. I was so convinced you were the one. I could never love someone who has so little faith in me. Screw you, Anthony. You're just as big of an asshole as Blake Havers."

I take my keys and purse and run downstairs to pack my bag. It's time for me to go home. I get halfway down the stairs before I hear the unmistakable sound of breaking glass, and it transports me back in time.

I'm a twelve-year-old girl climbing out of my bedroom window. I hear shattering glass and the screams of my mother as she puts up the last fight of her life. My father yells at her, calling her a whore and she tells me to run to Kat's.

I feel disoriented; nothing is as it should be. I climb into the closet and crawl deep into the corner. I bury my face in my hands and sob.

The minutes pass like hours. The house is silent as I hide in the closet like a terrified child. I finally get my tears under control, but my stomach is in knots. I feel physically ill. The fiery burn of bile rises in my throat and threatens to spill from my mouth. I make a mad dash out of the closet and into the bathroom just in time to empty my stomach. There isn't much to lose since I ate very little today.

I wash my face and focus on packing my bag, grabbing my essential bathroom items and several changes of clothes. I hastily toss my things into a bag and breathe deeply. At the bottom of the stairs, I try to gain the courage to take the twelve steps up because I have no idea what will be waiting for me when I get upstairs. Will he still be in a rage? I refuse to repeat the mistakes of my mother.

I take the steps one at a time, reach the landing and listen intently. All I hear is the crash of the surf as it smashes against the sand. Most times, it's a soothing sound, but tonight it sounds angry. The waves are loud and furious, just like Anthony. The wind blows through the open door, and a chill runs down my back.

I glance around to see what had been broken but find nothing out of place. My eyes are drawn to the beach, where I see the silhouette of a man. I can tell it's Anthony by the sheer width of his shoulders, and the fact that no one else would have access to his private piece of paradise. He's sitting on the sand, facing the water with head is in his hands, and his elbows are on his knees.

My first instinct is to run out and wrap my arms around him, to comfort him, but who will comfort me?

I take one last look before I walk into the garage and out of Anthony's life.

CHAPTER SEVENTEEN

The drive to my house takes an eternity. I turn on the radio and listen to whatever is playing. I choose a station for their emphasis on love songs. I listen with a heavy heart to songs like "Bound to You" by Christina Aguilera and "Somewhere Only We Know" by Lily Allen. I completely lose my shit as I pull my car up to the curb in front of my house, just as John Mayer's "Dreaming with a Broken Heart" plays.

The words of the song crush my heart and strip my soul. How could I have been so wrong? How does a man hold back your hair while you puke your insides out and then call you a whore less than eight hours later?

I slip slowly from the driver's seat and walk up the cement walkway. I'm going to have to remember that the only person I can count on is me. I put my key in the lock and open the door. The house smells musty from being closed up for so long. There must be fifty pieces of mail on the floor. I'm supposed to do a change of address, but I never get around to it. In the end, it's a good thing I didn't find the time.

I shut the door behind me and walk over to the couch, and

collapse. I allow myself fifteen minutes to wallow in my sorrows. Once I finish, I pull my phone out of my pocket.

There are over twenty missed calls from Anthony. I delete without listening to any of the voicemails. There are many texts, but I don't have the energy to read them. There is nothing he can say at this point. The last call on my phone is Kat. I go to the kitchen to get a Diet Coke from the refrigerator, then back to curl into a ball on the couch.

I look at my phone for a minute. Avoiding the compulsion to read Anthony's messages, I type a quick text to Kat.

Hey, Kat, it's Emma.

Oh, sweetie, are you okay? Where are you?

I'm home. My home. Please don't tell Anthony.

He knows, honey. He called us and asked us to check on you. He said you wouldn't answer your phone or his texts. He guessed that you went to your house. What happened?

I don't want to talk about it. Can we talk tomorrow? I just want to go to sleep.

I'm on my way. Hang in there. I'll be there in twenty minutes.

Please don't come. I'm going straight to bed. Let's meet at Java Joes for breakfast around ten o'clock tomorrow morning.

All right, but I'm worried about you.

I'm okay. I'll see you tomorrow. Love you!

You're full of shit, Emma, but I'll respect your decision. I'll meet you at Joe's. Love you!

Night

I end my text and turn off my phone. I'll have to get another charger tomorrow, because I left mine at Anthony's. It's hard to get all the things you need in a few minutes. You just run. It's the classic fight-or-flight response, and I was trained for flight because I saw what happened when you stayed to fight.

I spend the next two hours deep cleaning the house. Roxy is coming tomorrow to see the space, and I want it to show well. I have always used cleaning as therapy. If the house is spotless, then my life is not going so well.

I throw my sheets in the washing machine and make a cup of tea. My stomach is still upset, and I'm hoping the chamomile has a soothing effect. I sit on the couch and run the day through my head again.

Everything was going well. Granted, I was sick this morning, but he was so sweet. What person cares for you so well, then turns on you like a rabid dog? Who would've thought we'd be where we are now, given how fabulous we came together in the shower this morning? It was beautiful, and I have no idea how I'm going to get through this.

I sit in a daze—thoughtless and zoned for hours. When I finally pull myself back to reality, it's past midnight. I drag my tired, depressed self to my room. I quickly put fresh sheets on the bed and climb under my down-filled duvet, trying to find comfort in something.

I toss and turn for hours. The last few months of Anthony's and my relationship play over and over in my head. I don't know where his aggressive behavior came from. He has been more possessive lately; however, I've never seen him respond with violence.

Blake Havers was a complete idiot today. We've only had a platonic relationship. I went to a restaurant opening with him once, and I attended the last food and wine festival with him, but that was six months ago.

I toss my body around, trying to find a comfortable position to be in. I'm used to sleeping with Anthony's body next to mine, his arms cradled around me. My head fit perfectly under his chin. His hips tucked up close to my bottom.

Rolling to my side, I stare at the only picture I have of my mom. We are leaning against a tree in the park. I'm eleven in the photo. I had a disposable camera that had one shot left, and I asked a stranger to take the picture. I stood behind her because I was taller and wrapped my arms around her neck, with my chin rested on her shoulder.

My dad had been gone for weeks, and things were happy and carefree. It was a warm summer's day. We went for an ice cream cone before we went to the park to swing. My mom loved to swing. We would sit side by side and see who could go higher. I loved jumping from the swing as I propelled it forward. My mom would never jump; she said she was afraid of breaking something. In hindsight, that strikes me as funny. She avoided something that had little risk of hurting her, yet she stayed in the place that would eventually kill her.

I drift off to sleep with the thoughts of sunshine, ice cream, and my mom's smile on my mind.

I WAKE up to the sound of the doorbell. I look at the bedside clock and see the time is 8:30. The doorbell continues to ring, and I'm disoriented from lack of sleep. I slip on my fuzzy pink slippers and slowly make my way to the door. I unchain it and unlock both deadbolts before I throw it open. Whoever is behind this door better back off because I'm in no mood to deal with people today.

"What?" I yell. I find Anthony standing in front of me. He has two cups of coffee and is several feet back from the door. His posture is nonthreatening, and I imagine he stepped back from the door as soon as he heard the locks being thrown.

"Emma, please don't close the door. I'll stand here, so you're not afraid."

I look behind him at the taxi idling by the curb. "What are you doing here?"

"I had to see you. It took everything in me not to come over last night."

"Shouldn't you be at the airport? You really shouldn't be here."

"My flight is leaving in a few hours. Please don't push me away. I came to apologize."

"Okay, have a pleasant flight." I close the door but hear his plea through the door. He sounds like a wounded animal.

"Please, baby, I love you. My heart is in your hands. You can crush it or make it soar," he pleads.

"I can't do this right now. I didn't sleep well last night, and I have to meet Kat in a little while. Thanks for coming by, Anthony, but I don't have room in my life for this."

"Please, Emma, I'm begging you. Sit on the porch and drink coffee with me. I brought your favorite. I'm not asking for you to let me in. I'm begging for a few minutes of your time. I'm leaving for four days, and I don't want to leave things like they are." I open the door, and he looks at me with soft, pleading eyes. I waiver long enough for him to approach me. He sets the coffee down and pulls my stiffened body into his arms. His lips are on my hair and I relax slightly before I push him away.

He steps back and looks at me with sadness. I sit on the top step and wait for him to sit next to me.

"Say what you need to, and then you should go to the airport." My eyes are blurry as I fight the tears that threaten to spill. I swipe at the lone tear that escapes. Before I can reach it, Anthony's thumb softly brushes it away.

"I'm sorry. I know I scared the hell out of you yesterday. I scared myself, too. I've never reacted like that. My only excuse is that I'm so in love with you I can't think clearly." He leans his head to each side of his shoulder as if trying to crack his neck. "I wasn't mad at you. I was mad at myself for blurting out something I knew I shouldn't have. I know you, and you're a loyal, honest woman. When I saw Blake touch you, I saw red. He spewed his ugly words, and I couldn't stand for him to say those things about the woman I love."

"Are you referring to the same things you said when we got home? You're just as bad as he is—worse because you had all the power to hurt me, and you used it." I reach down and pick at the pink fur on my slippers.

"I know, and I'll never forgive myself. I'll give myself no excuse. I'm a thirty-four-year-old child. I got jealous, and I misbehaved. Please don't throw away what we have because I was an idiot."

"What did you break?" I watch him cringe as I ask the question.

"I threw a glass, but it wasn't at you. I was mad at myself. As soon as the words came out, and I couldn't take them back, I was furious with myself. I threw it in the sink, and it shattered. I can only imagine where that took you. I'm so sorry. You know I'd never hurt you." He reaches for my hands, but I pull them away. His shoulders visibly sag.

"You hurt me, Anthony. You scarred my heart, which will take some time to heal. You damaged the trust we built together."

"I understand that. I'll do whatever it takes to build your trust in me. I told you already you're the only one for me. I knew it the day I saw you, and I know it now. There will be no others."

I look out at the waiting cab and giggle. "That's going to be one hell of an expensive taxi ride."

"I don't care about the cost of the taxi. I care about you, and I don't want to leave you."

"Why are you going to Dallas, anyway? You seem stressed, and you aren't sharing any information with me."

"I didn't want you to get stressed. I have to check out the two stores in Dallas because there have been some discrepancies in the books. A lot of money is unaccounted for. Then the incident at Ahz happened, and now, this. It's been a shitty week."

"We used to live together. I was supposed to be your partner," I tell him. I can't look into his eyes because if I do my heart will break. Maybe I judged him too harshly.

"We still live together, baby. Come home. I need you with me. I screwed up, but I promise it won't happen again."

"Let's talk more when you get back. I don't want to add to your burdens."

"Why do I feel like you're not coming home?"

"I need some time to think. This morning, I was never going to talk to you again. See how far I've come." I smile up at him.

"Please come home, baby. I have to go, but it's going to be so hard to leave you. I haven't spent more than a day without you in my arms or my bed. Can I kiss you goodbye?"

I lean into him; he draws me like a magnet to metal. His lips brush gently against mine. His kiss is tentative like he's testing the waters. I melt into him, burying my nose in his chest. His fingers gently lift my chin as his lips fuse with mine. My heart is pounding out of my chest, and I don't know if it's from love, hope, or something else. I open my mouth to inhale and feel his tongue enter. His kiss is slow and passionate. There are a million words said in this kiss. My hands slide up his chest to wrap around his neck. He deepens the kiss, our tongues dancing. It's a sexy dance, like the Samba or the Tango. The world around me disappears, and only he and I exist. We linger in the abyss for several more minutes before he pulls away.

"I want to take you into your room and make love to you. I can't right now because I have a plane to catch, but I want to. You don't know how much I want you." He looks down at his pants. My eyes follow to his crotch.

"Hold that thought until Wednesday," I say. We both stand. He grabs my head and pulls me in for another mind-bending kiss.

"Are you coming home, baby?"

"I'll think about it. We have a lot of unresolved issues. Keep kissing me like that, and I can't think of anything but how nice that feels."

"Go back to bed. I'll text you from the airport. I have to run. I love you."

"I have to meet Kat for coffee soon, and then Roxy is coming to see my house."

"She's coming to your Malibu house? Wow, I didn't know we were subletting rooms. I said that we were having problems with money in Texas, but we are far from destitute," he teases.

I give him a playful punch before I reply. "That's your house. I'm talking about this house."

"We'll talk about what's mine and what's yours when I get back. I have to go. I'll miss you. Emma, and I'm so sorry." He holds my hand until the distance he travels pulls us apart. I watch from the porch as he enters the cab and pulls away.

CHAPTER EIGHTEEN

I rush into Java Joes and see Kat sitting in the corner with two coffees in front of her.

"You're late," she says as she watches me with a guarded expression. "Don't tell me you were up early this morning having makeup sex."

"No, I wasn't. We didn't have time. He had to catch a plane to Dallas."

"What am I going to do with you? What in the hell happened? Damon spent over an hour on the phone with Anthony last night. It didn't sound good."

"It was awful. I ran from him like a twelve-year-old girl. Sometimes I wonder if I'll ever be able to put that scared little girl to bed. Anthony isn't much better than me; he's a thirty-four-year-old boy who is used to getting what he wants. His mom spoiled him, and he thinks the world is his oyster."

"Sounds like he's perfect for you, then. He doesn't want the world, Em; he wants you. You're his oyster, and it's shucking season, girlfriend." Her shoulders shake as she laughs.

I laugh at her joke, but sober as I remember what sent me

running yesterday. "He threw a glass last night, and I lost my mind. I hid in the corner of the closet and cried. I only left the closet to throw up."

"Maybe you should go see Dr. Lydell again. She's helped you through a few rough patches. If the stress is making you physically ill, then you need to see her."

"Yeah, I think you're right. I'll call her tomorrow."

I RUSH AROUND, trying to get a power cord for my phone and make it back in time to meet Roxy. I see her in my mind as a bleached blonde who looks somewhat like a white Grace Jones—a badass chick in leather and silver studs.

I pull up in front of my house with about fifteen minutes to spare and take a few of them to plug in my phone and check my messages. There are several from Anthony.

I arrived in plenty of time. You are right; it was the most expensive taxi ride ever. It was so worth it. I love you, Emma. I'll call you tonight. See you Wednesday.

A few minutes later.

I didn't hear from you yet, and I'm worried you changed your mind. Are you avoiding me again?

Later still.

Worried, please text or call me.

The last message was about twenty minutes ago.

My phone was dead. I was having coffee with Kat. Things are fine. Stop worrying. Roxy will be here shortly, so call me when you get to Dallas.

I'm relieved. You had my heart palpitating. I will call you as soon as I land. Have a good afternoon, baby. I love you.

The doorbell rings just as I read his last text. I open the door and see a brown-haired, brown-eyed girl staring me down.

"Hi, I'm Roxy. Are you Emma?" She holds out her hand for me to shake. I tilt my head in confusion. She is not the Roxy I was expecting. This girl looks sweet and normal. I figured anyone who hangs out with gay men all day would have to have a bit of an edge.

"Yes, I'm Emma. Come on in. Let me show you the house." I step aside to let her enter. She's about my height with ample breasts, a tiny waist, and narrow hips. She's top-heavy for the rest of her. It looks like she may topple over any minute.

"I was excited to come here today. I live in Burbank right now, and it's just too much of a haul to get to Trax. This would be about a twenty-minute drive, so it's perfect."

"Chris and Trevor told me you work at Trax. How is that?" I raise my eyebrows. It's a strange job for a pretty, straight girl.

"I love it. The men don't bother me, and the women are harmless. It also pisses my parents off, so that helps." Her eyes scan the house as we move farther into the living room.

I take her on tour around the place. It doesn't take us long; it's a two-bedroom bungalow. I show her the room that would be hers, and she gets giddy. I've never seen a girl so excited about an en-suite bathroom. She enters the small walk-in closet and looks around. There are still a few of Kat's items hanging about. While she is looking at the space, I notice a brown box in the corner. I walk around her and pick it up. The top falls open, and several unmentionables fall out.

We stand aside and look at the floor. I burst into laughter as the last vibrator rolls out of the box.

"Well, that settles it. I want this room. If it comes with toys, then I'm in. However, I'll have to pass on that whip-looking thing and the handcuffs. I don't mind a little spanking or some breath play, but I haven't tried the whole BDSM thing yet." She looks at me as if to see my reaction. I'm still stunned by the plethora of sex accouterments lying on the floor.

"Well, these belong to Kat. I'll have to let her know she left them here." I giggle at the thought of that conversation. "You'll have to order your own sex store." I gather up the selections, place them back in the box, and back into the closet.

"Every girl needs a good B O B and a large supply of batteries," she says. I'm glad that she has a good sense of humor. That could have gone so differently.

"I call mine Roger Rabbit," I tell her. The reference is to the vibrator I have, and Kat always told me I looked like Jessica Rabbit. "So, here's the deal. The house is paid for, so my roommate will need to cover the utilities and the gardener. That runs about five hundred dollars a month. It's a steal of a deal for this neighborhood. I originally thought I wouldn't be around very much, but things have been stressed in my relationship, and I'm not sure how it's going to pan out." I pause for a moment, thinking about the last few days.

"That's cool. I rarely bring my men home, but if I wanted to bring someone over, would that be a problem?"

"No, as long as they don't end up living here. I ask that you keep your sexual activities in your room. I expect my housemate to be neat and tidy. I'm not a clean freak unless I'm stressed. I take my frustrations out on the mop and vacuum."

Her eyes scan the room. "So, I guess you're having a bit of a bad day? The house is immaculate."

"Yes, it's been a hectic week. Listen, it's lunchtime. Do you want to get a bite to eat so we can get to know each other a bit more?" I look at her expectantly.

"That sounds like a great idea." She twirls around once more before we leave the bedroom. We gather our stuff and make our way to Abe's Diner a few blocks away.

Roxy and I spend the next hour learning about each other. Her name is Roxanne Somerville, and she is the middle child of a disappointed set of parents. They expected more from her than she expected from herself. She reminds me of Kat in many ways. She is candid and open. I can see why Chris and Trevor thought she would be a good fit.

I knew I liked her the minute the box of sex toys spilled all over the floor. She didn't freak out. She just laughed and joked about it. By the end of lunch, I tell her that if she wants the room, then it's hers. She lets out a big whoop that startles our fellow diners. Maybe I wasn't so wrong with my preconceived notion of who she is. She is a girl who can kick ass, but her demure look threw me off.

She plans to move in right away. I hand her a spare key, and we go our own way. I feel good knowing there will be someone living in the house. This house means a lot to me. It's the last gift my mom gave me. After she passed away and they read her will, it came out that she had taken out a large life insurance policy on herself. I think she always knew she would die young. She set up a trust for me, and I inherited the money the day I turned eighteen. It was enough to buy a car and put a sizable down payment on my house. I paid the remaining balance off with the money I earned escorting.

I walk several blocks back home with my mind full of thoughts and emotions. Anthony's presence this morning changed everything for me. I was so convinced we were finished. I was preparing myself for months of heartbreak and healing. He shows up, and I melt. What does that say about me?

Dr. Lydell is definitely on my list of things to schedule. I need to work out these crazy thoughts that are surfacing. My emotions are all over the place. I pull my phone out to make the call. I know her office is closed, but at least I can leave a message.

I see my phone, and I've missed Anthony's call, showing he is in Dallas. *He's hitting the ground running but will catch up with me later.* The second message is from the *Los Angeles Times* reporter asking me to call him so we can set up a time to meet.

With all the drama over the last few days, I almost forgot about the crisis Ahz is facing. I call the reporter to set up a personal meeting tomorrow. I'll take him to the restaurant where he'll ask the questions, and we'll have lunch. After that, I'll give him a behind-the-scenes tour of the club.

My notebook is full of things I have to do. I browse through the list, checking off the items I've completed, and make a new list of the things I haven't been able to get to. I've sent the invitations for the prom to over seven hundred people. I used an acrostic poem.

People dressed in uncomfortable clothes.

Ripping their seams on the dance floor.

Oh... my gosh, the punch is so good.

Maybe prom will be fun.

You are cordially invited to travel back in time to your prom. If you loved it the first time, then relive it. If you didn't go, don't miss your second chance. If it fell way below your expectations, you know you'll love the prom at Ahz. We are pulling out all the stops to make sure this is a night you will remember.

I'll need to check on the RSVPs that have come back. Trevor is in charge of that. He's a bit of a control freak and wants to know the who's who that will be attending. He's like our very own Perez Hilton.

Back in the house, I think about my prom experience and what I'll be wearing. Anthony promised to match his Chucks to my dress. I don't plan to make it easy for him. I rummage through my closet to find the hot-pink dress I wore to the only dance I ever attended in high school. I have no idea why I kept the dress, but I think it's because it has sentimental value. I attended homecoming with

Chris. It was such a glorious night, with no pressure and no expectations, just a lot of dancing.

I take a picture of the dress with my phone and send it to Anthony.

Start looking for the perfect match.

I found the perfect match the day I met you. What are you doing?

I was planning my outfit for prom. It's a big day in a girl's life.

If I could roll my eyes, I would. Unfortunately, he's not around to see it.

You aren't going to make this easy, are you?

Have I made anything easy for you?

No, but you've made it worth it. I'll get on it. I love you. I gotta run.

I put my phone into my back pocket and smile.

CHAPTER NINETEEN

I spent last night in my house. There was no point in going to Anthony's since he wasn't there. I arrive at work bright and early to find Trevor waiting for me by the elevators.

"So, how did the meeting go with Roxy?" He looks nervous, but it's not like I'd stop liking him if I didn't like her.

"Great, she's in like Flynn." I snap my fingers with my statement.

"I knew you'd like her. She's so much fun. A little on the wild side, but I think she's still rebelling against her parents."

"Yes, she said something about pissing them off. I like her a lot. I think she is moving some of her stuff in today." I shrug my shoulders, not sure if that's the case. She has a key and will come and go as she pleases.

"Nice. I came out to meet you because I wanted to show you the number of responses we've received. You sent out seven hundred invites, and we've had four hundred and thirty-five 'yes' responses. These are all couples or parties of two. This is going to be huge! Is there anything I can do to help you?" The idea has taken off. Many people are looking forward to reliving their prom. Who would've thought?

"No, I need to get through today. I have a meeting at noon with the reporter from the *Times*. That should be fun." False humor strains my voice. "I also have to leave early today because I have a medical appointment. However, I think I have it all under control."

We walk into Ahz and back to where the offices are located. I no longer have to share a space with Kat. I have my little windowless box in the corner of the first floor. It's not much, but it's mine, and I love it. I toss my jacket and bag under my desk and check my voicemail.

The first message is from Anthony, wishing me a good day. I replay it twice to hear his voice. The second message is from the vendor producing my decorations for the prom. Everything is being shipped today. The last message is from Tom Wakefield. He's the reporter for the *Times* and wanted to confirm our noon appointment.

I pick up the phone and call Kat.

"Hello, this is Katarina," she answers in a sweet voice.

"Hey, Kat. It's Em. Can you come and see me?"

"Sure, I'll be right down."

Her office is at the opposite end of the corridor. I imagine our men planned it that way so we would get some work done. I hear her heels clicking along the tile floor. It doesn't take her long to make her way down to my space.

"What's up?" She bounces into my room and plants herself in the chair in front of my desk. She always seems to be happy these days, and her smile is contagious.

"I wanted to let you know I rented your room to the girl from Trax. You still have some things in the closet. Do you want me to box them up for you?" I raise my eyes in question. Does she even remember the box?

"There shouldn't be much. Just a few sweaters, and I think

there's a box of college books in the corner." She thinks the box in the corner is filled with college books. That's funny.

"Funny you should mention the box. I picked it up, and its contents spilled all over the floor. Imagine my surprise when three dildos, two vibrators, a set of handcuffs, and a flogger came falling out." I stare at her and wait for her reply.

Her cheerful face goes from smiling to jaw-dropping dismay. I watch as the blood rushes from her lower extremities directly to her face. She opens and closes her mouth several times before she talks. "Holy smokes. That was our book club box. I thought I grabbed it when I packed my stuff. I honestly thought the box in the closet was filled with textbooks. How embarrassing. Damon had bought props just in case we wanted to try some things in the book. Oh, shit," she gasps. I watch as the realization of what I'm telling her finally sets in.

"No big deal. I just wanted you to know that Roxy would only take the room if it included the toys." I try to give her a straight-faced look, but I can't help the laugh that bursts from my lips. "Just kidding. I mean, the stuff fell out, and she mentioned keeping it, but she wanted the room, regardless. You'd like her."

"I'm mortified. What did you do with the stuff? I hope you tossed it."

"Never! How could I throw all that inspiration away? It's in my trunk. I was going to bring it in and display them in a tidy row on your desk." It gives me great pleasure to make Kat squirm.

"Thank God you're feeling generous today. Things must be going better with Anthony." She tries to dodge the subject by redirecting everything to me.

"We're working through it. He's in Dallas, so we're communicating through phone calls. He needs to get his jealous streak under control, and I need to stop reverting to that twelve-year-old girl."

"Have you ever asked him about his past relationships? Maybe he has some skeletons in his closet, too." Kat looks around the room. "I'd love to stay here and discuss sex toys and boyfriends, but I have stuff to do, girlfriend." She lifts herself to a standing position, turns, and walks out my door.

I never really considered he might have some old wounds that haven't healed. It's worth asking him.

I SPEND the rest of the morning organizing the prom and looking through the guest list. We are going to need a lot of spiked punch.

At eleven forty-five, I walk to the front entrance of Ahz to meet with Mr. Wakefield. I lean against the wall and shoot Anthony a text message.

I am waiting for the reporter to arrive. What are you up to?

Meetings. Good luck today.

Thanks. Is everything okay?

Yes. Just working, I'll talk to you later. I love you!

Okay, I love you too.

"Are you Emma?" the blond-haired man asks. "I recognize you from your photos."

My photos? That can't be a good thing. My picture has been taken many times, but the most recent was at the food and wine festival. This has to be the reporter. "Are you the reporter from the *Times*?" I ask.

"I'm sorry, I should have introduced myself. I'm Tom." He offers me his hand. I give him a gentle shake before I open the door to Anthony Haywood's restaurant.

"I'm Emma. Welcome to Ahz. I thought we would have some lunch, and then we can take a tour. How does that sound?" I look over my shoulder as I lead him to our reserved table. He smiles brightly as he takes in the restaurant.

"Absolutely perfect."

"Have you ever dined here?" I'm pretty sure he hasn't, but it's always good not to assume anything.

"No, this will be the first time." His eyes take in the warm atmosphere. The restaurant is not busy, so that he can see it clearly without the distraction of a crowd.

"Well, then you're in for a treat." We take our seats, and I tell him about Anthony Haywood's. "The restaurant has a standard menu, but the chef's fresh choices are offered as well. I'd opt for one of those. They're always amazing. They purchase everything from the daily menu fresh that morning."

We both select our meals, and I settle in for the inquisition.

"First, I want to make sure you know everything we talk about this afternoon is on the record. Do you understand?" He puts a tape recorder on the table and presses record. He pulls a small notepad and paper from his jacket and places it next to his water glass.

"Yes, I know." My heart races, and I figure it will be tough. It's my first time representing Ahz, and I want to do a good job. I look at him expectantly.

"Let's get started. Ahz and its half-owner Anthony Haywood have received more bad press lately. He is featured in several pictures that were recently taken at the Los Angeles Food and Wine Festival. Rumor has it he was defending your honor. Is this true?"

"I have no comment about Mr. Haywood's personal life. Contact Mr. Haywood if you want to know anything about his life outside of Ahz." He's coming out with his guns blazing.

He places a few newspaper articles in front of me. The first one has the headline "She's a Whore!" written across the top. "This picture tells a story, Ms. Lloyd. It shows one of the leading food critics out cold after your boyfriend decked him, and you have no comment?"

"Mr. Wakefield, I invited you to talk about the accusations that have been thrown at Ahz. Anything beyond that is off-limits." I shake my head back and forth. It's a natural reaction for me when I think someone is an idiot.

"Nothing is off-limits when it comes to the news, Ms. Lloyd."

Just as he asks another question, our salads come. We spend a few minutes eating before he continues.

He talks with his mouth partially full. I can see the chicken from his salad move around inside his cheeks. "My researchers couldn't dig up anything official yet, but word has it you are an escort for hire." He swallows and then takes a drink of water to wash it down. "You're a stunningly beautiful woman. I can see how you could make a lot of money doing that."

What a jerk. I shake my head. "I work as the PR representative for Ahz, Mr. Wakefield. Shall we talk about the current allegations, or would you rather eat lunch and take a tour?"

He takes a minute to look at me and then jots something on his notepad. His writing is chicken scratch. I can't decipher a single letter. "The car that plowed through the crowd at the Nokia Theater had a nineteen-year-old driver with a blood-alcohol level of .21. When they pulled the driver from the car, she sported a stamp from the clubs at Ahz."

"Yes, that seems to be the consensus. Is there a question, or are you reminding me of the facts?" I'm trying to be professional and stick to the facts, but he has a callous, arrogant attitude, and I don't like him.

"Is it a regular practice to allow underage kids to drink at Ahz?"

"We follow all state and local guidelines concerning drinking age."

"Isn't it risky to have *Eighteen and Overnights*?" He picks up his pen and jots down a note. I wonder if he does this to break my concentration.

"*Eighteen and Overnights* are becoming a club standard, Mr. Wakefield." His question is one I've asked myself repeatedly.

"Please call me Tom. Regardless of the industry standard, an incident like this can put an entire brand out of business."

"I believe the police are investigating the allegations, Tom. Additionally, Ahz has hired an independent investigator to look into the accusations. Do I have to remind you that no one affiliated with Ahz has been charged with any crime?" I roll my neck, trying to get the kinks out.

Tom wipes his mouth with his napkin and places it on his plate. "That was a great chicken salad. I've never had one that was quite as satisfying." He pushes his plate to the side and looks at me. "Clearly, you and Mr. Haywood have an open relationship. Our partners in Dallas have been checking up on Mr. Haywood since he arrived yesterday. He obviously has a type." He stares at me; it's as if he's baiting me and waiting for my reaction.

"I don't know what you're getting at, Tom. Would you like to clarify?" I look at him like he has two heads.

"I always say a picture speaks louder than words." He reaches into his pocket and draws out a picture of Anthony escorting an attractive redhead into one of his restaurants. His hand is resting intimately on the small of her back. I'm left speechless.

"Are you ready to take the tour, Mr. Wakefield?" I have to get up and move. My eyes keep drifting to the picture he left in front of me. *Who the hell is that girl?*

"I have caught you off guard. That was not my intention. I apologize."

"You were trying to knock me off balance. So what? Maybe I'll get angry and divulge some information that would give you a story. I'm sorry to disappoint you. Whatever Mr. Haywood does in his spare time is his business; we're not married. I told you before; if you have personal questions to ask about Mr. Haywood, you should set up an interview with him. Would you like his assistant's number? I can get it for you before you leave. Shall we go?" I bet my face is the same color as my hair. This man gets under my skin.

I spend the next hour walking him through the club and show him the ID scanners and how every guest who enters gets a stamp. They scan the stamp at the bar, and it tells the server if the customer can order alcohol or not. The bar light flashes red if the stamp is an under twenty-one patron. They can order only one drink per person at a time. It's not a foolproof plan, but it is effective, or it has been in the past. Damon has been using this technology for years in his other clubs.

When we arrive at the ground level, I usher him to the door.

"This ends our tour. Do you have any other questions?"

"No, I'm impressed with the club and your security measures. I guess we'll have to see what the police end up finding."

"Yes, I think they're almost finished with the investigation." I take my business card out of my pocket and hand it to him. "Please contact me if you have additional questions."

He takes the card from my hand and holds on too long, so I yank it back from him.

"You are a beautiful woman, Emma. It was my pleasure meeting you."

Ew. I wish I could say the same. "Take care." I turn abruptly and head straight for my office. I have about thirty minutes before I'm expected to be at Dr. Lydell's.

CHAPTER TWENTY

It's been over a year since I last saw my therapist, and I arrive with only a minute to spare. I usually make an appointment around my mom's death anniversary, but I thought things were going better this year. In the end, I guess I still need her.

I check in at the receptionist's desk. Instead of waiting for a few minutes, I'm escorted right into her office. She sits comfortably in a leather chair and motions for me to take a seat.

"Emma, it's good to see you. You look well. Tell me what brings you in today." She lowers her glasses so she can look over them. She's an older woman, probably in her early fifties, and has salt-and-pepper hair and baby-blue eyes. She has a thin, wiry-looking body, one that looks like it belongs to a long-distance runner.

"Nice to see you, too. As you know, this is the time of year I struggle the most. I thought I was doing well this year, but I seem to be falling apart rather frequently. I have a boyfriend, and we fought on Saturday. He did something that sent me running and hiding in his closet."

She writes a few notes down and looks at me. "What sent you running?"

"He questioned my past, and when I walked away from him, he threw a glass. The sound took me to a dark place." I shudder as I remember hiding in the closet.

"Why did you run away?"

That's odd; of all the questions she could ask me, she asked why I bolted. "I don't know. I guess I was tired and didn't want a confrontation."

"That's not necessarily normal behavior for you, is it? I remember you being a feisty girl. You were always setting the rules. I believe you told me once, 'It's my way or the highway.'"

"No, you're right. I usually fight back. I usually define the rules, but it's different with Anthony. He's a big man with a forceful personality. I've fallen into a more submissive role than I'm used to." I think about that for a few minutes while she writes more notes.

"Is he threatening or abusive in any way? Do you feel unsafe?"

"No, of course not. He's an amazing, gentle man. He's bossy, but he is always looking out for me. He's the best man I know." Wow, that is quite a revelation.

"Okay, so why the broken glass?" Her eyeglasses get pushed down, and she looks directly at me.

"Why did he break it? Or why did I cower from it?"

"Tell me about both. I'd like to hear you work it out."

"He broke it because I was walking away from him. I have been pulling back a bit, and I think he felt threatened. I've never been in love, and the vulnerability of giving someone so much power scares me. I can understand his frustration at me walking away. A reporter showed me a picture of him with his hand on a girl's back, and I wanted to throw a glass."

"Is your relationship exclusive?"

"Yes, we live together." Well, we used to. I think we do. Oh, hell, I don't know.

Her eyes lift in surprise. "That's a big step. What else is happening?"

"I haven't been feeling great, and I think it's making me act like a crazy woman. One minute I'm laughing, and the next, I'm crying. I'm tired all the time, and I have been under the weather lately." I touch my tummy, remembering the times I've thrown up in the last week. "I've had some stomach bug. I think if I could just start feeling better, I'd be okay."

She sits there for a minute. The office is silent as she seems to work something out in her mind. "Emma, are your periods regular?"

What a strange question for a shrink to ask. "No, I've been considering changing from the mini-pill to the shot. I've had a lot of breakthrough bleeding the last few weeks, and I'm moody as hell."

"Emma, I'm going to ask you to make an appointment with your regular physician. I think you may be pregnant. You have classic symptoms. I don't want you to panic, but I think you need to at least rule it out." She pauses and stares at me.

I feel like my world turned upside down. I can't be pregnant. I take my pill regularly. Leave it up to fate to make me fall into the failed group. A three-percent failure rate doesn't look too bad until you're the one that's pregnant. "Holy shit. I can't be pregnant. I promised myself I'd never end up like my mom. If I got knocked up and he feels forced into marriage, how am I supposed to live with that?" I burst into tears.

Dr. Lydell pokes her head out the door and asks her receptionist to call her next patient and delay their appointment. She is going to need more time.

"Emma." She hands me a box of Kleenex. "You live in a very different time. You get to choose whether to have a baby or not, to get married or not. You have options. You don't even know that you're pregnant yet, so don't get all worked up about it. You can get a home test, although I think the blood test would be your best bet."

"I feel anxious." I tear the tissue in my hand to shreds.

"You always seem to feel anxious. My notes indicate you suffer from severe anxiety at times. I can prescribe something for that, or we can take a different approach. I want to address the glass breaking. Sometimes it's best to immerse yourself with the thing that scares you the most." She reaches into her Rolodex sitting on the table next to her and pulls out a card. "This may seem silly, but a lot of my patients have visited this place and found it to be very therapeutic."

I look at the card she hands me, and it says,

The Smash Shack
- Throw your frustrations out the window
- Break the cycle of anger
- Crush anxiety forever

On the back is an address. I lift my eyes to hers and smile.

"Yes, it's unconventional, but I think it will do two things for you. First, it's going to help with any anger you feel. You can write names on plates, cups, whatever, and then throw them at the wall or the window. It's symbolic of letting go. It's time for you to let go, Emma. Second, you're still reverting to glass breaking; it's the one thing that terrifies you and stalls your recovery. Force yourself to see it can be a positive thing. It's a way for you to break the hold that your past has on you."

I consider her suggestion for a few minutes. I mentally write names on white plates. Mr. Wakefield, the stupid redheaded girl in Dallas, my dad (Daniel Lloyd), the grandparents I never met, the drunk driver, and Blake Havers.

"I think it's a great idea. I have a complete list in my head already."

She smiles a big, toothy grin. "Emma, let me know how things are going. Shoot me an email or make a follow-up appointment. I honestly think you're doing okay. You recognize behaviors you don't want to repeat, and that's healthy. You're protective of your boyfriend, which means he's important to you. These are all positive things."

"I feel better now that I talked to you. Do you think I should ask

Anthony about the girl? I think the reporter was trying to get a rise out of me, and he succeeded."

"I can't tell you what you should do, but I believe everyone deserves the benefit of the doubt. You keep mentioning a reporter. Who is this? And why are you talking to reporters? That sounds stressful all by itself."

"My boyfriend is Anthony Haywood. I work at Ahz as the PR representative. You may have seen something in the paper about an underage drunk girl and an accident downtown. I was addressing that."

"Wow, that's fabulous. Not the allegations, but the job and Mr. Haywood. He's a very handsome man. He's older than you, right?"

Why are older women so focused on the age difference? "Yes, he is ten years older than me, and he is quite handsome." I feel warm and fuzzy thinking about him.

Dr. Lydell rises from her chair, showing that our session has finished. We walk to the door together. She invites her next client in, and I pay my bill before heading home.

CHAPTER TWENTY-ONE

At the bungalow, I hurriedly enter the house to find Roxy in the kitchen, cooking something that smells great.

"Hey, what are you making? That smells amazing." I walk into the kitchen and find her making something with cheese, meat, and green chili.

"It's just a quesadilla. I like them meaty and spicy, like my men. Do you want one?"

"Yes, but not spicy. I have a problem with spicy." I grab my stomach and make a retching sound.

"Enough said—just meat and cheese for you." She tosses some ingredients into the pan. A few minutes later, we are sitting at the table, inhaling our food.

"How is the move-in going?"

"Just about finished. I just had clothes to bring over. One more trip, and I'll be done. What were you up to today?"

"I had to meet a reporter at Ahz, and then I had an appointment this afternoon." The mention of an appointment makes me think of the next one I have to make. Holy shit, I forgot about the possibility that I might be pregnant. How did I let that slip my mind? I think

I'm just trying to pretend it's not happening. How long can I live in denial?

"That's right, you work at Ahz. Doesn't Damon Noble own Ahz?"

"It's a co-branding between Anthony Haywood and Zenith. They combined the letters A-H-Z and came up with Ahz." I still think it's so smart. It was so cool when I told the reporter welcome to Ahz today.

"Anthony Haywood?" Her eyes light up. Most people know who he is. "Do you know him well?"

"I hope so; he's my complicated relationship." I see her eyes grow wide. "Do you know him?"

She turns her head away from me before she answers. She gets up and walks to the kitchen. "No, I can't say I know him." She tidies the kitchen. "How long have you been dating?"

"Several months. It was a love-at-first-sight kind of thing. He's a great guy. However, the reporter showed me a picture today with his hand on a woman's back leading her into the Dallas restaurant. I felt an enormous amount of jealousy, seeing his hands on another woman." I open and close my fists as if I'm getting ready to punch someone. "That's what our fight was about over the weekend. He hit someone who touched me inappropriately. He was mad that I'd been out with that person on one occasion. It was a business meeting, not a date. Anyway, I don't know why I'm telling you all of this."

"That seems out of character for Anthony."

I turn to look at her closely. "You said you didn't know him."

"Oh. I don't. What I meant to say was, that doesn't seem like the thing a man of his stature and position would do."

"I didn't understand jealousy and rage until this afternoon when I saw that picture."

"Do you think he's stepping out on you? That seems out of character, too. Isn't he a public figure? He'd have to know he wouldn't get away with it." She cleans the frying pan and puts it away.

"I don't think he would, but he has a lot of stress in his life right now."

"Give him the benefit of the doubt, but ask him, so you're not wondering."

That seems to be what everyone is telling me these days. "What are you doing tomorrow? The reason I ask is that I am going to this place called The Smash Shack to release my aggression. I'm going to invite Kat, and I thought you might want to meet her."

"I know it well. I only work Friday through Monday, so that should be great."

We agree to meet there after I get off work at five. I leave Roxy in the kitchen and walk to my room to call Anthony.

"Hello, babe, how was your day?" his voice sounds tired.

"It's nice to hear your voice. I miss you."

"I miss you, too. I didn't sleep well last night. I'm used to having you in my bed, and I was lonely."

"Lonely enough to replace me?" I listen patiently as he digests the question.

"I can never replace you. You still don't get it. How many times do I have to tell you you're the one? Your name is tattooed on my heart. Maybe I have to tattoo it on my forehead; that way, you'll know it's you I love."

"No tattoos. I was just feeling jealous when the reporter showed me a picture of you and a redhead walking into your restaurant. He was trying to upset me. It worked, but I put on my poker face and didn't let that affect the interview. It went well, by the way."

"I wasn't having any meeting with a redhead. You're the only redhead for me. I probably just opened the door for someone." There is a thoughtful pause in our conversation. "I knew you would do well in the interview. How did the tour go?"

"Great, I showed him the lengths we went through to make sure we didn't serve minors. I think I won him over."

"I bet did that the minute he looked at you. Now I'm jealous."

"Speaking of jealous—how's your hand?" I think back to the break in his skin from punching Blake.

"I'm good. It's a little sore but healing. It was worth it. Not the fight we had but seeing that slimy worm laid out on the floor. I guess we made the front-page news. I saw it, and I'm sorry about the headline. I've called the paper and asked them for a public apology."

"We'll see if that happens," I say sarcastically. "How are your meetings going? You seemed quite busy when I texted you earlier."

"Things are moving along more slowly than expected. I may not be home Wednesday but will probably be an additional week."

My heart has just plummeted into the pit of my stomach. That's ten days apart. How am I supposed to get through that? "I don't know what to say." I can feel my throat close with that achy emotional feeling you get right before you cry.

"I have to straighten this stuff out. I met with the accountants today. I meet with the lawyers tomorrow. Yesterday, I met with the private detective I have on your case, and he thinks he found some of your family."

The mention of my family stops my need to cry. "I have a family?" I ask in awe.

"You just might. I'm trying to get him to move more quickly, but it takes a lot of digging to exhume a past." I hear the unmistakable sound of a can of something being opened.

"Started drinking early today?" I question teasingly.

"Just a diet soda. Do you want to fly down here and stay a few days?" I can hear the longing in his voice.

"I can't. You put me in charge of this silly prom, and I'm swamped. I didn't work all day today because of the interview and my appointment. I feel like I'm behind."

"I'm disappointed, but I understand. How did your appointment go?"

Should I tell him I might be pregnant? In a split-second decision, I choose to wait until I know for sure. He has enough on his plate right now. "It went well. I'm going to break dishes for therapy tomorrow. I'm taking Roxy and Kat with me. Roxy's the new roommate, and she seems pretty cool."

"Where do you plan to break these dishes? I hope not at the restaurant." His voice sounds slightly concerned.

I begin to laugh as visions of me chucking plates in the kitchen of Anthony Haywood's run through my mind. "Of course not. There's a place called The Smash Shack that offers aggression services. We're going there, and then I think I'll take everyone out to dinner."

"I'm jealous. They get to have your time, and I get nothing."

"Hey, you went to Dallas. I'm still here. You have my heart, and they only have a bit of my time." He can't see me roll my eyes. He is so spoiled.

"How is everything at the house? I hope it's still standing."

"I don't know. I haven't been back there since I left Saturday night." There is silence on the line.

"I figured as much. You never mentioned the flowers I sent, so I figured either you didn't get them or you're still mad at me."

"I'm sorry, I didn't know. I'll stop by tomorrow morning. It would be weird to be at your house when you're not there."

"Damn it, Emma, it's *our* house—not *my* house. Go home to our house. Paint the walls pink if you want. Just do something, so it feels like home to you. You seem to have one foot in and one foot out of the door all the time. You're going to have to decide. Are you in this relationship or out?" His voice rises with every word spoken until he is yelling at the end of the sentence.

"Don't yell at me. You're not here, and you're the only thing that feels like home. You can be such an ass sometimes." I hang up the phone and turn off the ringer.

What do you do when your life feels like it's going downhill fast? Usually, I'd break out the wine and toss back a few. However, I might be pregnant, and wine is now off-limits. I would also call reinforcements. I pick up my phone and text Kat.

SOS, *I need you now.*

On my way! How much wine do we need?

No wine, but Rocky Road ice cream is a must.

Quart or a gallon?

Buy out the store.

I put my phone down and change my clothes into my flannel pajamas and pink bunny slippers. Some people have comfort food. I have comfort clothes. Well, I also like ice cream.

I settle on my bed and wait for Kat. I look at my phone and see a missed call and text message. In the end, he's right. I have to commit or let him go entirely. I can't imagine my life without him. He makes everything brighter and more beautiful. The sky is bluer because he stands under it. The air is sweeter because he breathes it. I pick up my phone and text him.

I'm in.

In what?

In love with you. I'm sorry. I'm hormonal, but I am seeing the doctor this week. Forgive me?

Yes, go home and sleep in our bed. I want to smell you on my pillow when I get home. I love you, Em.

I'll go tomorrow after I pick up the paint to match my prom dress. I think it's an excellent color for the kitchen, don't you?

Whatever you want, babe. I can overlook any color as long as I'm looking at you. I'm sorry I yelled.

It's okay; we're both under a lot of pressure. I love you. Let's talk tomorrow night. Okay?

Okay, until tomorrow night then. Love you.

Kat walks into my room just as I open my computer to search for signs of pregnancy. In one hand is a gallon of Rocky Road and in the other is a bottle of merlot.

"I brought both, just in case you changed your mind." She climbs up next to me in bed and hands me a spoon and the ice cream. "Spill it."

I bite my lip, trying to figure out how to subtly tell her my news. I weigh my words, but in the end, I just blurt it out.

"I may be pregnant." It comes out in a steady whoosh of air. I feel better just vocalizing the possibility.

She grabs the ice cream out of my hand and pulls off the lid. She doesn't even wait for the spoon; she just digs her fingers in and grabs a glob. I watch in disgust as she shoves it into her mouth. This is the Kat I grew up with, the one who will do anything to lighten the tension.

Through a mouthful of melting chocolate ice cream, she opens her mouth. "Are you sure?" she asks.

I tilt my head at her and scrunch my mouth and eyes, giving her my "are you serious?" look. "The word *may* indicates that I'm not sure. Dr. Lydell told me my symptoms all lead to pregnancy. Then again, it could be anemia or cancer, so who knows?"

She licks her fingers and looks at me. "You seem to be taking this pretty well. Why is that? I would have expected you to be buried in bed and in a fit of tears."

"I can barely stop myself from wrestling you for that bottle of wine. The only thing that stops me is that I may be pregnant. What am I going to do?"

"Get a pregnancy test. Then figure it all out. Have you told Anthony?" At the mention of Anthony, I cry.

Kat puts the ice cream on the nightstand and hugs me. She smashes my face into her chest and whispers all the things I want to hear. Things like *it's going to be okay*, and *we'll get through this*.

"I think I'm in denial. I don't want to be pregnant right now. I want some time with Anthony before I have his baby. I want his babies, but I just didn't want them now. Is that selfish?"

"No, I think we all want to plan the perfect life, but sometimes fate has a way of stepping in." Kat pets my hair, and I like the way it feels. Anthony does the same thing, and it always soothes me.

"Yeah, well, if fate were a woman, I'd slap that bitch. Hasn't she given me enough to deal with in my life? Don't you even say you only get as much as you can handle because that's bullshit, and you know it." I watch as Kat opens and closes her mouth. She tweaks her lips to the side and lifts her eyes. This is her thinking face.

"When are you going to tell Anthony? He has a right to know."

"There is nothing to know right now. I have to make a doctor's appointment and get a blood test. Dr. Lydell didn't think a pee test would be beneficial since I've been spotting. She just said the blood test would be definitive. Even if I took the pee test, I'd have to get the blood test to confirm."

"I'd be peeing on a stick if I were you." Kat looks past me at the wall. "Besides the bad timing, how would you feel about being pregnant?"

"I feel like I failed Anthony and myself. He's a good man, and he would marry me in a second if I were having his child. I don't want to be that girl. I want him to marry me because he loves me and because he can't live without me."

"I think we have already established that he loves and wants you to be his. I remember him saying something like he couldn't breathe unless you were in the room."

I use one hand to brush away my tears and the other to push my rogue curls out of my face. "He isn't having too difficult of a time breathing. He was seen with another redhead yesterday. He wasn't even gone a day, and he was ushering another girl to dinner. It's like he's repeating our first date with someone else." I breathe in a ragged breath and try not to cry again.

"That's crap, and you know it. He would never cheat on you. Whatever is going on with you, we need to get it under control before you lose your mind. That man is whipped when it comes to you."

"You're right. I've just been off. I'm pregnant, or I need a different method of birth control. Speaking of birth control, I need to stop taking it, right? It's bad for the baby, correct?" I think about the little life that may be growing inside of me. My hand unconsciously reaches down and rubs my stomach. I'm already in love with the baby I'm not sure I'm having. I think I may be losing my mind.

"When are you going to go to the doctor?"

"I have to call tomorrow. This reminds me, I have an assignment of sorts from Dr. L. She wants me to smash plates at The Smash Shack. She thinks it'll be therapeutic."

"I've heard of that place. I'll go. I have a few names to write down myself."

We make plans to go after work. We'll drive together and meet Roxy there.

"Have you heard anything about the investigation? I was going to ask Anthony, but we started disagreeing, and I got sidetracked."

"Yes, I think we are off the hook. Her boyfriend admitted to drinking with her once they left Ahz. They couldn't get a drink with our tight policy and left to drink elsewhere. I just found out right before I came here. Damon was going to call Anthony as soon as I left."

I feel such a sense of relief. "Why couldn't we have that information before I met with the creepy reporter? At least now they will move on." I reach over and take the container with the partially melted ice cream into the crook of my arm and dig in. I still need chocolate.

"Are you doing better now? I can stay the night if you want. We can snuggle together like we did when we were kids, but I have to draw the line at you drooling on the pillow."

"No, it's okay. You talked me off the ledge. I'm good. And I'll have you know, Anthony has never said a thing about my drool." I give her my best indignant look. My eyes shift sideways, and my head tilts. She laughs and hugs me.

"See you tomorrow, Em. I'll show myself out. Oh, and I met your roommate earlier, and she seems nice."

"I met yours, too, and I like him. Have a good night, Kat. Thanks for being there."

She blows me a kiss as she walks out of my room. I look down at the bucket of ice cream I set aside to hug Kat. It's more like chunky chocolate milk. Just looking at it makes my stomach roll. I climb out of bed and venture into the kitchen to dispose of it.

"Hey, are you okay?" Roxy asks from her perch on the couch.

"Yeah, just a tough day. What are you watching?" I walk to where she is sitting and take up residence on the other side of the sofa.

"Just reruns of *Fresh Prince of Bel-Air*. You can change the channel." She reaches out to hand me the remote.

"No, I love Will Smith." The theme song plays in my mind. I sit down just in time for a commercial.

"The Law Offices of Somerville and Sloan," the commercial says. I look to Roxy and find her staring back at me. "A relative?" I knew Somerville sounded familiar. It's a large law firm in downtown Los Angeles. They cover everything from ambulance chasing to corporate law.

"Yep, that's my dad. You can see why he's a disappointed parent. We were supposed to either become lawyers or marry well. I did neither, so they wrote me off."

Wow, I thought I had it bad. "Do you have any siblings? I know what it feels like to be a disappointment to a parent. My dad never liked me," I matter-of-factly tell her. The more I say it, the less it seems to bother me. Maybe I am moving past my horrific childhood.

"Yes, there are three of us. Roseanne, Roxanne, and Reanne. My parents thought they were so cute and clever. My oldest sister married a partner. My younger sister is in law school. I hang around gay men." She shrugs and goes back to looking at the television.

The way she describes her life makes me laugh. She is funny.

"I'll be here tonight, but I'm going back to Anthony's tomorrow. Will you need anything?"

"No, I'm fine. I start back to work on Friday. I took yesterday and today off to get moved in and organized," she says. "I've got your cell number if I need anything."

We spend the rest of the evening in companionable silence. Every once in a while, Roxy or I burst out in laughter when Carlton, Will, or Ashley does something crazy. Before I doze off, I decide to head to bed.

CHAPTER TWENTY-TWO

I wake to the sound of my cell phone ringing. Right Said Fred plays "I'm Too Sexy." That's Anthony's ringtone. I stretch and reach for it. He is way too sexy for just about everything.

"Hello," I answer in a tired, gravelly voice.

"Good morning. Sorry to wake you. I just didn't want to start my day without saying hi. I have meetings all day, and we probably won't get to touch base until tonight."

"Come home. I'm tired of sleeping alone," I whine.

"I wish... how did things go with Kat last night? I talked to Damon, and he said you two were hanging out."

"She brought me ice cream because I was down. I'm good now. There's nothing a gallon of Rocky Road can't cure. I'm sure it's going straight to my ass."

"I love your ass—I miss your ass. Actually, I miss everything about you."

"I miss you, too. Tell me how things are going." I sit up against the headboard and settle in for our conversation.

"I have a meeting with the accountant. There are some fairly large discrepancies, but they haven't been going on for very long.

The loss is negligible in the scheme of things. We'll still be able to eat," he teases.

"It's awful that people you trust are stealing from you." The idea of anybody doing something wrong to him pisses me off.

"Yes, it's awful, but hey, at least we got good news about the drunk driving situation. Damon says they are wrapping up the investigation today. That's one thing down."

"That was very stressful. Hopefully, things will go more smoothly in Texas and you can come home early."

"I'd love that, but I don't see that happening at this point. I'll get home as soon as I can. Speaking of home, did you decide to go back to our house?" I can hear the hope in his voice.

"When I get back from breaking dishes and dinner with the girls, I'm climbing into our bed in your house."

"Emma, it's not my house. I'm sharing it with you. We're a team now."

"Well, then I guess I should sign over half of my house to you. That way, we both have a vested interest in staying together."

"That sounds like a fabulous idea. I'll get my lawyers on it right away. Listen, babe, I've got to run. I have an early meeting. I'll call you tonight."

Did I just offer him half of my house? What did he mean he was going to get his lawyers on it? Can he draw up papers to take half of my house? The funny thing is, I'd sign them. I've always held on to this house like it's a bar of gold, and yet if Anthony wanted half of it, I'd gladly give it to him. I slide out of bed with a smile on my face. The thought of sharing everything with him fills me with joy. Then it hits me again—I could be pregnant. I'm so torn between feeling giddy that a piece of Anthony is growing inside of me and scared of the implications.

I don't want someone to be with me just because I'm having his kid. I remind myself that he wants to be with me now, and he has no idea I'm possibly pregnant. I wrap my arms around my tummy and give myself a hug. I can hear us telling his parents. His mom would probably say, "That's why you don't try it before you buy it." In the end, I think they'd be happy because lord knows, "They aren't getting any younger."

I shower, dress, and head off to work. The day seems to drag. An hour is the same amount of time every day, so how come some hours seem longer than others? By the time five o'clock rolls by, I'm itching to leave.

I hear Kat's heels on the tile floor and her keys jingling in her hand. I reach in my drawer to get my bag and race out to meet her.

"Are you ready to break some dishes?" she asks.

"Yes, ma'am, let's blow this joint."

"I thought you might want to see this." She hands me today's edition of the *Los Angeles Times*. "Turn to page three."

The headline to the article is Ahz is Red-hot. I read through the article and see Mr. Wakefield was pleasantly kind in his writings about Ahz. He called me professional, competent, and red-hot. *Well, Mr. Wakefield, this red-hot girl is taken.* Flattery will get you nowhere. He describes the elaborate measures Ahz has taken to ensure underage drinking doesn't occur. It's about the closest thing to a stamp of approval one can get from a paper. I feel good about his interview. Maybe I won't write his name on a plate after all.

We climb into Kat's car and head for The Smash Shack. She is still driving the orange Charger Damon gave her. "Are you going to keep this car, or do you plan to get a new one?" I look around the vehicle. It's ten years old, but it's virtually brand-new. I peek over at the odometer, and it just passed 12,000 miles.

"Damon wants to trade both of the cars in for new Mustangs, one convertible and one hardtop. You know me; I'm happy to drive whatever." She keeps her eyes totally focused ahead of her.

"I have a doctor's appointment on Friday. It was the earliest they could get me in."

"Did you buy a pee test? I don't know if I could wait until Friday."

"No, I finally concluded it's not a terrible thing if I'm pregnant. Even if I bought a pee test, as you call it, I'd still have to wait for official results."

"I'm dying to know. You swore me to secrecy, but it's so hard keeping something like this to myself. I could be an aunt, and I am missing valuable days of shopping for baby stuff."

"Yes, and you might not be an aunt, so don't rush me. I'm wavering between absolute fear and happiness. There are so many unknowns. The first is whether I'm knocked up."

"All right, Friday it is." We pull up in front of The Smash Shack. Roxy is waiting patiently in front for us. She's leaning against the front window wearing a pair of low-hung jeans and a crop top. Her belly piercing catches the light and sparkles.

"Hey girls, are you ready to break some shit?" she asks.

We all shout, "Yes" at the same time. I see our reflection in the window. One blonde, one redhead, and one brunette; you couldn't have picked three different-looking girls.

As we enter the building, I can already hear the sound of glass breaking. I stop and catch my breath. Both girls flank me and stop. Kat knows my history, so she knows what this is doing to my insides. Roxy, on the other hand, probably just thinks I'm crazy.

"I don't know if I can do this." My hands sweat, and my breathing becomes erratic.

"Doctor's orders, Emma, you're doing it." The girls each take an arm and walk me to the front desk.

"Welcome to The Smash Shack," a perky little pink-haired girl says, and she asks us to sign in. "Which one of you is Emma?" Her eyes travel from face to face, looking for someone to claim the name.

"That's me." I give her a narrow-eyed questioning look.

"A Mr. Haywood called and said to tell you he loved you and that all the stress reduction is on him. Something about him causing most of it, anyway." She looks to me as if searching for some type of confirmation.

"Now if that's not true love, then I don't know what is," Kat chimes in. She pinches me in the side as she speaks.

"Ouch." I back away and out of her reach. "He's just protecting his dishes at the restaurant. He thought I was going to chuck plates in the kitchen at Ahz."

"I can still see you doing that. On a bad day, I've seen you toss anything that was in your way." Kat smiles at me. She's probably remembering the time she thought she lost my favorite pair of earrings. I picked up my jewelry box and flung it at her. All the jewelry spilled everywhere, and as fate would have it, the earrings in question lay at her feet as if saying, "I'm right here."

The pink-haired pixy leads us to a private room. There is a back table full of cups, plates, and saucers. Sharpie pens in all colors litter the table, as well. In front of us is a cinderblock wall. Faceless people of each gender are painted in various places on the wall. All skin colors and hair colors are represented. All you need to do is imagine a face, and you're set.

Kat walks to the table and picks up a plate. She writes the name Mara on it and sets it aside. She picks up a plate and pen for each of us. Roxy takes her plate, writes the name Eddie on it, and places it off to the side. I look at my plate for a minute and eventually scribble the name Daniel across it.

"Let's do this together, girls." I hand safety goggles to Kat and Roxy and lead the way to the yellow line that's painted across the floor. It's a safety line to avoid stray glass splinters that might pop back at you.

We line up in a row, and I count down from three to one. I find the blond-haired male figure on the wall and picture his face. As I shout the final number, the plates fly. The crashing of glass against the wall startles me at first, but then I laugh.

"What's so funny?" Roxy asks.

"I don't know. It's just that it's not as scary when you're the one doing the throwing. The sound of breaking glass sends me running, and yet here I am—throwing glass—liking the sound."

We walk back to the table to get more plates. Roxy tries a cup. We write the names of people who have done us wrong or things that have held us back. In the process, we toss all of those fears away. I take one last plate and write the name Blake Havers on it. I look to my right and see Roxy write creepy lurker on her plate.

We step up to the line and slam the last bits of frustration into the wall. I take my phone out of my bag and snap a picture of the debris lying on the floor and send it to Anthony.

I turn to Roxy and ask, "Who is the creepy lurker?"

"There has been this guy that has been across the street staring at the house. I wonder if he's a homeless guy, but he's dressed nicely, so I didn't think so. Have you seen him before?"

Kat and I look at her like she has three eyes. "No, what does he look like? Are you sure he's staring at the house?"

"He's tall and slender. He's dressed nicely, but I can't make out his facial features. He was wearing a baseball cap. I walked onto the porch and stared him down, and he left."

Kat shakes her head. "Don't mess around with that. Call the police the next time he shows up."

I leave their conversation as my phone beeps. I have a text.

It looks like you had a lot of therapy. How did it feel?

So much better than I thought it would. I think it was a great idea. We probably put you in the poor farm with the number of plates we broke.

It's not possible. I'm glad you found it helpful. I could break a few plates myself. However, I've learned my lesson and will resort to screaming in a pillow in

the future. You can be the official plate thrower in the family.

I think I'll pass. Maybe we can have a scheduled day a month to come here and break things. I miss you.

I miss you too. I'll talk to you later. Call me when you get home.

I head back to the girls and herd them out onto the sidewalk. I take one of their arms in each of mine and lead the way to the Lily Pond. We walk into the little hole-in-the-wall with the best egg foo young known to man.

We decide to eat family style. We order the egg foo young, of course, chicken with cashews, and shrimp with lobster sauce. We eat until we are ready to bust.

The server brings the bill with three fortune cookies. I snag everything before anyone can get to it.

"Okay, you have to answer a question before you get a fortune cookie. Who wants to go first?"

Roxy raises her hand. "I'll go. What kind of question?"

"Whatever I want to know." I think for a minute before I ask, "Roxy, have you ever been in love?"

"Nope, hand the cookie over." She lays her palm flat in front of me. I place the cookie in her hand. "Make sure you eat the cookie before you read the fortune, or it won't come true," I warn.

"Kat, when is the wedding?" It's not a good question because she tells me everything, anyway, but I'm hoping she has some new info.

"No plans yet. If it were up to Damon, it would be yesterday, but I'm just getting used to living together. I'm not sure I'm ready for a joint checking account yet."

"Wait. You're marrying Damon Nobel, and you don't want to have your name added to his checking account? Are you nuts?" Roxy asks.

"Our relationship has never been about money. I couldn't care less. I have enough. I live in an amazing house with an amazing man, and he's not going anywhere. There's no rush. Besides, there seems to be a fight over who will be my maid of honor." She makes a funny face at me. "Chris wants to wear the satin. He says he's got better legs than you."

"He's so full of it. He doesn't shave his legs. He can wear satin to the prom. He has to stand down for the wedding." I rock my head back and forth and give her a funny face back.

"Prom? Aren't you a little too old to go to prom?" Roxy asks.

"I never went to mine, so Anthony decided we're going to hold one so I can experience that rite of passage."

"I never went to mine either. My dad didn't want me to date anyone he didn't vet first." She looks off into the distance as if she's reliving a moment in time. "I'd have gone with Bobby Anderson if I were able to attend."

"Can you get a week from this Saturday off? You can join us for prom. Maybe we can even find Bobby Anderson. I'll look into it."

"He's probably married with three kids by now. I'll still come. I assume Trevor and Chris are going to be there, right? They're my biggest tippers, so if they aren't at Trax, I might as well not go. I love those boys."

"You have less than two weeks to find a dress for it and a date if you don't want to go stag. I'll try to find Bobby, but that's a pretty common name."

"You don't have to find Bobby. Last I heard, he was working for LAPD. I'm not sure he would even remember who I am."

"Well, we'll work on it. It's time for fortune reading. Has everyone finished their cookie?" I pop the last bit into my mouth and chew. "You first, Roxy."

She unfolds her fortune and busts out laughing. "The fortune you seek is in another cookie."

"I don't believe you!" I take it from her and read it myself, and it says exactly what she said. "That is the funniest thing I've ever read. Kat, you're up."

She looks at her fortune and melts a little. "You're guided by silent love and friendship around you."

"I love that one. Okay, it's my turn. Mine says... Love is not for the weak of heart." I tuck my fortune into my wallet as I take my credit card out to pay for dinner. I may have to look at it to remind me of how much I love Anthony when he drives me crazy. Maybe I should give it to him to remind him of how much he loves me.

"That is so true. If someone had told me how much I would go through to get to where I am with Damon, I might have turned and ran. Now that I went through it and survived, I'd do it all over again. He's worth the journey."

"Okay, girls, time to go. Thanks for breaking dishes and breaking bread with me." I sign the charge receipt and tuck my card back into my wallet. "I'm going to my beach house tonight. It'll be the first time I stay there alone. Keep your phones close just in case I need some support." I hug my oldest friend first and then embrace my new friend next. Kat gives me a ride to my car, and I am off to Malibu.

CHAPTER TWENTY-THREE

The last few days have passed by quickly. The first night alone in the house was a little spooky. It's amazing how many sounds you hear when another individual doesn't distract you.

I found two vases of flowers next to the gate when I came home the first night. Since then, he has had them delivered to the office so I don't miss them. Everywhere I go smells like fragrant blooms of roses and lilies.

We have talked every night this week. I fall asleep to him telling me how much he loves me, and I wake up to him telling me to have a nice day. Everything seems to be going so well.

Until the appointment reminder came in, I completely put the idea of a pregnancy out of my thoughts and worked on the guest list.

The new numbers are in for the prom. We have over six hundred confirmed couples. We are going to fill the third floor to capacity. The decorations will go up Friday night after the close of business. I'm so excited. It's not because it's the prom, but more so because I pulled it off. I wasn't happy when Anthony dropped this in my lap. I know he did it so I could prove to myself I was capable of more than fetching coffee and proofing ads. He's a sneaky man.

Just as I reach for the phone to call Kat and tell her I'm heading out, it rings.

"Hello, this is Emma. How may I help you?" I answer, using my most professional voice.

"Hi, Emma, it's Tom Wakefield."

Great, just what I need. "Hello, Mr. Wakefield, what can I do for you today?"

"I was just calling to see if you read the article?" There is silence on his end.

"Yes, I read it. Thank you for taking the time to visit and see beyond the rumors."

"I was hoping maybe we could meet again for coffee. Since you indicated Mr. Haywood's private life is his own business, I assumed you don't exclusively see each other."

My mouth drops open as I look at the phone. It's not like I can see him through a handset, but I'm shocked he'd be so bold as to call me at work. "I'm flattered, Mr. Wakefield. Unfortunately, I can't accept. We do see each other exclusively."

There is a moment of silence on the other end. "How does that work for you, Emma? You stay exclusive, and your boyfriend trots all over Dallas and Phoenix with another redhead?"

"I'm not sure what you're talking about, Mr. Wakefield. Anthony is in Dallas taking care of business, and I don't like what you're inferring."

"You may not like it, but that doesn't mean it's not happening. I'm sending some photos to your email now. If you change your mind about coffee, call me."

The ping of an incoming email sounds just as he hangs up. I debate whether to delete the emails or open them. You can't keep running from the things you don't want to deal with. My finger hovers over the email that says, "While you were away." I have an internal battle, and the curious girl wins. I push the button and watch as the pictures materialize.

There are at least ten of them. They start with the picture of his hand on the small of her back. I know they are at Anthony Haywood's because of the A-H engraved on the door handles.

Picture number two shows her face, and it stuns me. She is so similar looking to me, it's unreal. My hair is a deeper red, and my face is a little thinner.

Picture number three shows her standing by a car, and he is holding the door open.

Picture four shows her kissing him on the cheek.

Picture five is dated yesterday. It shows the girl with her arm slipped through Anthony's. They are in a parking lot. There are circles on several license plates. I enlarge the photo and see all the cars have Arizona plates.

I can't look at these anymore. I have to get to my doctor's appointment, and what I've seen has rocked my world. Not only is he with another woman, but he has also lied to me about where he's at. There is no excuse for that. I know things have been stressful for a few weeks, but he's been so loving while he's been gone.

I forward the pictures to my private email, gather my things and head out to see if I'm carrying a lying, cheating bastard's baby.

I PRESENT my arm to the nurse. One quick poke, and that's done. I look up at Dr. Clark. She has been my physician for years.

"It's too late for me to get results today, and the lab is closed over the weekend. I'll have them Monday morning; until then, we will assume you're pregnant. I can do an exam if you're eager to find out."

I contemplate my options and decide to wait. I have enough on my plate right now. I have a unique talent for compartmentalizing, and that's precisely what I plan to do about his situation. I'll pretend it's not happening until then.

"Monday is fine. I've waited this long, so what're another three days? In the event I'm not pregnant, I want to go on the shot, please. I don't want to have another scare like this. In the event I am pregnant, I'll need to hear about all my options. My relationship with the father is in question at this point."

"Okay, well, let's table this until Monday. We'll set you up an appointment. It won't take long to read the results, and we can make some decisions based on them then. Is there anything you need for now?"

"A bottle of red wine, but I suppose that will have to wait as well."

I set up my appointment for Monday morning and drive to Anthony's house. I make a cup of coffee and sit down at the breakfast bar. My laptop sits in front of me and calls for me to open it. I flip open the top and watch as it springs to life. The light shines brightly in the dark room.

Is this what I want? I look around me and see my surroundings. Anthony is everywhere. He's in the kitchen scrambling eggs. In the living room yelling at the screen when his team loses. I look out the glass doors at the surf to see the moonlight glimmering on the water. The white foam glows as it breaks on the beach. In my memory, Anthony emerges from the water after his daily swim. I wanted this. I wanted him.

I walk back to the breakfast bar, sit down, balance the cup of coffee in both hands, and inhale the aroma. I bring the cup to my lips and sip. It's decent but not as good as he would make it.

I open my email and click on the forwarded message. The pictures pop up like boils on a baby's butt. They're painful to look at. I enlarge them so I can analyze them one at a time. I gloss over the first five since I've already seen them.

Photo six shows him dining with the girl. She is smiling, and he looks like he's laughing. I can't see if anyone is with them or if they are alone. Is she the accountant? I'm trying to give him the benefit of the doubt, but the meeting looks cozy. He's wearing one of my favorite shirts. It's a baby-blue Henley. The cotton is so fine it almost feels like silk. Every time he wears it, I bury my face in his chest and rub my cheek up and down to feel the soft fabric on my skin.

Photo seven is almost like photo three.

Photo eight is of him entering a hotel. The photographer caught the image perfectly. I can see Anthony clearly, and the name of the property. Royal Palm Resort is printed on the door.

Photo nine shows him alone at the front desk.

Photo ten shows him alone at the bar in what appears to be the lobby.

I don't know who this girl is. I alluded to her in our previous conversation, and he said he was probably opening the door for someone. I don't feel like I can ask again without sounding like a jealous girlfriend. After getting on him about his jealous tendencies, doesn't that make me a hypocrite if I display the same behaviors?

I drink my coffee, even though it's turned lukewarm while I was studying the photographs. I decide I won't ask him about her, but I'll ask him how Dallas is. If he comes clean and tells me he's in Phoenix, then at least we can talk about it. If he lies to me, then I'm done. I sit back and wait for him to call.

I watch the surf from my seat at the bar. The warm ocean breeze coming through the open door is soothing to the soul. My hair whips around my face as I lean against the chair and think about my life. I've come to a lot of realizations this week. I learned I could overcome fear. I'm stronger and more capable than I thought I was. My motto was always "Fake it until you make it." I guess, in the end, I made it. My past can no longer define my future.

My weakest link is Anthony. He's my Achilles' heel. With him, I'm jelly. He speaks, and I get gooey all over. When he's near, I can barely think for myself. How can one man have such an impact on me?

The phone startles me from my thoughts. "I'm Too Sexy" plays two verses before I answer.

"Hello," I whisper. My voice is a whisper.

"Where are you at? I can hardly hear you." His voice gets louder as if he's trying to compensate for the softness of mine.

"Hold on." I walk into the kitchen. "Is this better?"

"Yes. How are you?"

"I'm good. I'm happy it's the weekend and plan to sleep in and then get my nails done in the afternoon. What are you up to?" I wait for him to give me some information. Maybe he'll say he had to fly to Phoenix and check on the restaurants. I pray silently he tells me anything that will give him the benefit of the doubt.

"Same old stuff. I was meeting with the accountant. I think I may be home Sunday. We'll see."

Here's the thing: she could be the accountant, but why wouldn't he say that when I asked about the redheaded girl? I have to think about this for a while.

"It's a warm and balmy day here today. How's the weather in Dallas?"

"Hot and humid," he says without a moment's hesitation.

"Good luck tomorrow. I'm going to take a bath and head to bed. It's been a long week. I'll talk to you tomorrow, okay?" The lump in my throat is just about choking the life out of me.

"Are you all right? You sound a bit off." His voice sounds concerned.

"Yes, just tired. Talk to you tomorrow."

"I love you, Emma." His voice sounds sincere.

When did he learn to lie so easily? Has he always had this skill, and I couldn't see it because love blinded me?

"Love you, too," I respond. I do love him, and it will take some time to get over that. Fate has dished me up another serving of bullshit. When I feel like my stuff is straight, she says, "Here you go, take this and choke on it." *Fate's a bitch!*

I close my laptop and descend to the ground floor. The spigot squeaks as I turn the bath taps on full force. I need a relaxing soak to clear my head and think about how I will handle it.

My natural reaction would have been to yell at him and call him a liar. That behavior hasn't worked well in the past, so I have to develop a new plan.

The bubbles cascade over my body, and I sink into the water until it gently laps over my chin. I wish I could stay in this bath the whole night. Unfortunately, I have to pack up my clothes and load my car. If Anthony is coming home soon, I don't want to be here for a confrontation.

FEELING CALM AND CLEAR-HEADED, I begin packing up my life with Anthony. I start in the closet first. I have a lot of clothes. I have no idea why I need this many pairs of jeans. I probably have at least twenty pairs, and I rarely wear them. I'm more of a dress girl. When I get settled, I'm going to have to clear things out. This is excessive.

I continue to make the trek up the stairs and into the garage, where I load my car. I shove shoes in every nook and cranny possible and put a suitcase full of cosmetics and bath supplies in the front seat.

I walk back into the house and look around. I was getting used to the idea that this place was going to be my home. Now I have to say goodbye. I wipe the silent tear that falls down my cheek and wish I could call Kat, but I wouldn't want to put her in a position to choose. She'd feel obligated to her future husband to tell him what's going on. She'd also feel her loyalty to me should take precedence.

I pick up my phone from the table in the kitchen and text Roxy.

Sorry for the back-and-forth confusion. I'm moving back in with you tomorrow. I'll be there fairly early and didn't want to startle you.

Thanks for the warning. It will be nice having you in

the house. The creeper was back today. I called the police, but he left before they came. I'd have freaked if the door opened unexpectedly.

That is creepy. I've never seen anyone lurking in the neighborhood, and I've owned the house for years.

Yes, it's weird. I'll see you tomorrow. We can talk about why you're running away again. I have to finish my shift, so I can't talk now.

I put my phone back on the table. Who is this man that keeps showing up outside? He started coming around the day she moved in. She's going to have to rack her brain to figure that one out. I never had a stalker before, and it's suspect that he showed up the day she did.

I walk back down to the bedroom and climb into bed. His pillow smells like him, and I inhale deeply. He is always fresh and clean, with a hint of citrus, and I'll miss him.

I think about my texts with Roxy. Am I running away again? Is this a pattern with me? When things get tough, I just run for cover? I don't think so. Usually, I fight back; however, I'm always in preservation mode. That may make me more self-centered than I should be. I'll have to think about that.

I WAKE WITH A START. My heart is racing, and I am covered in sweat. I was running in my dream. Each time I turned around, I saw a faceless person. Just before I woke up, he grabbed my arm, and when I turned to look at him, I saw Anthony. Is this my subconscious' way of telling me I'm indeed running?

I look at the clock and see I've slept longer than expected. I get up and throw on some clothes. I walk upstairs and start the coffee and open my computer and watch the emails rush in. The first in the queue is a message from Anthony.

Emma,

I've been away far too long. I booked the first flight I could. I'll be home tonight. Wear something sexy for me. I've missed you so much.

Yours,

Anthony

Wow, I wasn't expecting that. I'd hoped I'd have a few days to figure this out. Now he'll be here tonight, and I'll be gone. I don't want him to come home to an empty house. I want to get brave and talk to him. He deserves an answer, and I deserve the truth.

I shoot him an email back, hoping he'll get it before he boards the plane. According to his message, he should be arriving today around 6:30.

Anthony,

Come to Ahz for dinner. I'll reserve a private room for us. See you when you get here.

Em

I pour a cup of coffee and walk out onto the deck. It chokes me up to know I won't wake to this view every morning. I look out to the ocean and try to remember the last time I saw Anthony emerging from the water after his daily swim. Can I leave this all behind? Honestly, there is only one answer. It's yes, you can't live with a man who cheats on you and then lies about it. My pissed-off girl is back, and she's in the driver's seat for the day.

I stroll back into the kitchen, rinse my cup, and put it in the dishwasher.

The house is all locked up, and I'm ready to go. I walk to the garage door and look around me one last time before closing the door on my past. Seated in my car, I start the engine and head toward my uncertain future.

CHAPTER TWENTY-FOUR

I sneak into my house, so I don't disturb Roxy because she probably didn't come home until the wee hours of the morning. Most bartenders don't get out until well after two.

I haven't known her long, but I feel like I've known her forever. I'm sure that's why Chris and Trevor thought she'd be a good fit. She seems to have summed me up in the few times we have hung out.

It takes several trips between my car and the closet to get everything put away, but I finally have it all shoved back in its original home. The coffeepot is calling to me from the kitchen, and even though I shouldn't be drinking so much caffeine, I put a pot on to brew and sit down at the table with nothing else to do but wait.

What am I going to do about Anthony? I decided that I will show up to dinner with the pictures so when I can't talk to him, I can at least show him what I know.

A rustle to my left makes me jump. I was so caught up in my thoughts and I didn't hear Roxy enter the kitchen area.

"Good morning. I hope I didn't wake you." I watch as she walks over to the pot and pours herself a cup.

"Thanks for making the coffee. Do you want some?" She pulls a second cup out of the cupboard and waits for my answer.

"Yeah, that would be great. Black is fine for me."

"I know you don't know me that well, but do you want to talk? You have yo-yoed several times between houses lately, and I think maybe you might want a sounding board."

I stare at her for a minute. I'd rather talk to Kat because she knows me and my history. Since talking to Kat is out of the question, I'm happy to speak to Roxy. My computer is in the living room, where I left it when I arrived. Retrieving it and sitting back down at the table, I open the email with the photos. She shifts her chair to see the screen more easily and scrolls through the pics.

"You moved out because he was talking to another redhead some slimy paparazzi happened to conveniently take a picture of. Are you crazy? Did you even ask him about it?"

I'm shocked by her dismissal of his blatant disrespect for our relationship. "I asked him, and he breezed over the subject and disregarded the question outright."

"Anthony is not the cheating kind of guy. He's the commitment kind of guy," she blurts out and then looks at me like a deer caught in the headlights.

"Why is it you know so much about my boyfriend? You have slipped several times about what a good guy he is... blah, blah, blah. Tell me what I don't know, Roxy." I cross my hands over my chest and stare her down. She shifts uncomfortably in her seat before she speaks.

"First off, I want you to know I didn't know you were dating him when I moved in. I knew Katarina was connected to Ahz through Damon, but I thought you were connected through Katarina. I didn't know both of you were dating Los Angeles' most eligible bachelors." She sips her coffee and sits back in her chair.

"Go on. Tell me what I need to know." I feel like I'm going to be blindsided. Will she tell me she had a relationship with him? Does she know something that will help me work through my decision? Not only do I have an entire relationship to consider, but I also can't forget I may be carrying his child. What do I plan to do about that?

"I know Anthony. I've known him for years. He was engaged to my sister."

My heart squeezes at the mention of him being engaged. I feel like the ground just dropped out from under me. I grab for the table and hold on while the earth gobbles me up. He has never mentioned a former fiancée. He's never talked about any relationship. I just assumed he was like me, either a serial dater or too busy to date at all.

"Forgive me for being speechless, but I've never heard of a long-term relationship, not to mention a fiancée. Herein lies my problem: it's not the girl in the photos I'm concerned about; it's the sneaking around. He's supposed to be in Dallas, and yet, here he is at a hotel in Phoenix." I scroll back to the picture of him walking into the Royal Palm Resort.

"It's not my place to tell you Anthony's business, but I'm going to because I think you need to hear it." She scoots her chair closer to the table and closes my computer. I'm assuming she wants my full attention.

"Okay, I'm all yours." I lean back in my chair and get comfortable.

"Seven years ago, Anthony and Roseanne met at one of Damon's clubs. They both hit it off, and things went swimmingly well for a couple of years. Before I go into that, though, you have to get a good feel for my family. I told you my dad wanted boys to take over the firm. He had three girls. Imagine his disappointment when his oldest started dating a chef. Anthony had done well by then. He had a few restaurants, but nothing like the world domination of fine dining he has today. I think it was the situation with my sister that forced him to step up his game."

Roxy picks up our cups and walks to the coffeepot to refill them both. She sets mine in front of me and retakes her position next to me.

"My dad was an enormous influence in her decision to break his heart. He wanted all of us to marry his partners if we weren't going into law ourselves. Roseanne studied law, but she wasn't interested in being a partner. She liked the prestige of the degree but had an adverse reaction to working."

"What happened that broke Anthony's heart?" I'm completely caught up in her tale. I'm learning something about Anthony he didn't opt to share about himself. I kind of feel like a voyeur, looking through a private window in his life.

"We grew up very privileged children. Money was never an issue, and we never really heard the word no. Our parents had their thumb over us regarding careers and coupling, but everything else was fair game. We learned to live a life of excess, having closets full of Louboutin shoes and couture dresses. Anthony proposed to Roseanne on the second anniversary of their first date. He's romantic that way. He pays attention to the details." She pauses for a moment, and I take that time to gain my bearings. I don't enjoy hearing about him almost marrying someone else.

"Roseanne said yes. She was listening to her heart. Unfortunately, she had to listen to my father, and his voice spoke louder than Anthony's words of love. My dad reminded her that she lived the life of a princess. There was no way a chef was going to keep her in the lifestyle she was accustomed to. It didn't matter he had many locations already open; he'd need to make millions to compete with the picture my dad painted. In the end, my sister chose money and status over love."

I feel a tear slide down my cheek. I can picture Anthony's face as she broke his heart. I brush the stray tear away and tell her to go on.

"My sister walked into his restaurant the next day and handed him back his ring. Two weeks later, she married a partner from the law firm. The message to Anthony was, *you're not good enough or rich enough to hold on to me.* He begged her to come back but gave up when the wedding photo hit front and center of the *Los Angeles Times.* I think he took his anger and aggression and applied them to making his millions."

"What does your sister think now?" I am curious to know if she regrets throwing him over for a bigger fish.

"I don't know because I don't talk to my family. Knowing my sister, I'd imagine she thinks she chose poorly. If she'd just supported her man, she could've had it all. She seems happy enough. She gets the clothes and club memberships that are important to a woman who's empty inside. I'm happy he didn't marry her. He would've spent his entire life trying to please her and never succeeding."

I think back to dinner with his parents. Claire mentioned he'd brought one girl home before me. They called her Rose. I bet the girl was Roseanne.

"That's awful. However, I don't know how this has anything to do with my situation. I'm not tossing him aside because he's not enough for me. I couldn't care less about money. I'm done because I don't want to be that girl who is oblivious to her boyfriend's philandering. I don't want the press writing stories about how I overlook his dishonesty and infidelity because he's rich. I wouldn't have cared if he lived in a beach house or a flophouse. I'd have loved him, anyway." My eyes burn with the unshed tears I'm suppressing.

"All I'm saying is this, I haven't seen Anthony for many years, but I believe I know who he is. I don't think he's cheating on you, and if he's lying, it's for a reason he will reveal when he thinks the timing is right. He's not a deceptive man; he's a man who loves completely. If he's in love with you, there will be no room for anyone else."

I stare at Roxy for a minute and wonder if I just made a huge mistake. Am I finding him guilty before he even gets his trial? I'm so confused, and my feelings are so conflicted. I hug Roxy for taking the time to talk to me. I know it wasn't easy for her to tell me a story that wasn't hers to share, but I'm glad she did. I stand up and hug her again and then plod slowly to my room. I feel both emotionally and physically drained.

The pattern on the ceiling seems to change the longer I look at it. I have so much to consider. I rub my stomach and think about the little Anthony that could be growing inside my belly. Am I prepared to be a single parent? Am I prepared to end a pregnancy? The thought of aborting my baby makes me sick to my stomach. If there is a baby, they didn't ask for the parents they got; it's just the luck of the draw. I contemplate that thought for a minute. I, of all people, know you should never blame a child for conditions surrounding their birth.

At that moment, I realize if I'm pregnant, I will have this baby. I will love this child as my mother loved me, albeit I hope to live to old age to watch my child grow. I feel a huge weight lift off my chest. I know Anthony would be a great father, and even though we wouldn't be together, we'd co-parent perfectly. He is a good man, despite what we're going through.

MY PALMS ARE SWEATY, slipping slightly from the steering wheel as I turn into the parking garage at Ahz. The table should be set for tonight. The staff is always happy to accommodate you when you're dining with the owner. I slide my car into a spot in the first aisle and walk toward the entrance. I'm a messy mix of emotions right now.

Anthony asked me to wear something sexy, but since this is not the reunion he expects, I am wearing a pair of jeans and an off-the-shoulder purple tunic. I meander my way through the restaurant and into the private dining room. My watch shows it's six thirty. He should be here any minute. I almost get to the table when I hear the door open behind me.

My heart is in my throat.

He stands before me in a beautifully tailored suit, his five o'clock shadow giving him a rugged, scruffy *GQ* look. His blue eyes light up when he sees me, and I watch as he drops the briefcase from his hand and makes a beeline for me.

The air pushes from my lungs as he embraces me a bit too hard. His lips crush against my mouth, and for a moment, I almost forget why I'm here. I push against his chest, breaking the connection, and immediately say, "We need to talk."

His eyes open in surprise and disappointment washes over his face. He looks at me cautiously.

"Have a seat. I ordered us dinner. I hope you don't mind. I figured you'd be hungry when you arrived." He pulls out my chair and takes a seat beside me without saying a word. I look at his face and see the confusion in his eyes.

"I missed you. I'm so happy I'm home. I was lonely without you." He stares at me. I look into his eyes and see the fear. Is it fear of being caught, or fear that something significant has just happened and he hasn't a clue?

"I missed you, too. I think the reporter from the *Times* thought I was missing you as well. He sent me a bunch of photos, just in case I needed an Anthony fix. Sadly, you weren't missing me as much as I'd hoped. I had no idea how much it would hurt me to see you with another woman, but it destroyed me."

I grab my phone from my purse and set it on the table. I pull up the photos and put them to show as a slideshow. Picture after picture pops up. He seems surprised but doesn't jump to defend himself.

"It's not what you think it is. I'm not cheating on you." His voice is calm and almost monotone.

"It looks pretty cut-and-dried. She was with you almost every day you were gone. How long have you known her?" I can almost forgive a weak moment. He'd left on the heels of a major fight. Has he known her for a long time? Maybe it's me who's the other girl. I can't forgive him if she has been in his life for a while and he never told me. "Is she gone forever, or will I have to worry about her?"

What am I saying? He was with another woman. My question might lead him to believe we're still a couple, which is not the case.

"She's going to be around for a while, I think." A small smile emerges from his lips.

"You're a son of a bitch! How can you profess your love to me and then hook up with some young redheaded whore willing to spread her legs for you?" The accusation spills out of my mouth quickly.

I watch his lip twitch as he vacillates between laughter and anger. Anger finally wins.

"Damn it, Emma! You decided I was guilty, and now you're making me hang for a crime I didn't commit. Everything I do is because I love you."

"You love me so much you have to leave my arms and fall into the embrace of another woman who happens to resemble me. You know, I could get over the girl. It wouldn't be easy, but I could. I can't get over you lying to me about where you were. The entire time you were gone, you told me you were in Dallas, and yet there you are, walking into a luxury hotel in Phoenix. Is this where you slept with her? Did she travel with you? I bet you had a fabulous time." My face is hot from my fury.

He growls in frustration and combs his hands through his hair. "I'm done, Emma. I have loved no one as I love you, but I can't love someone who doesn't trust me. You've had one foot in and one foot out of the door since we met. When you decide you want to commit yourself to a relationship, let me know. I may still be around and have a small bit of love left in my heart for you. But until then, stay the hell away from me."

He pushes away from the table with such force, the water glasses tumble over and spill onto the floor. I'm left in shock. Somehow I'm to blame for his lack of integrity and inability to keep his junk in his pants.

"I can't let you leave without telling you I might be pregnant." I watch as the anger leaves his body. He stares at me. "I have an appointment on Monday morning to pick up my results." My eyes lower, so I can't see his face. I don't want to see how he feels about this news or see him look at me with hatred.

He bends over to pick up his bag, reaches, in and pulls out a manila envelope. He stalks toward me like a bull running at a matador. Slamming the parcel down on the table, he turns to leave.

"Text me the address of your physician. I have a right to be there." He storms out without another word.

I sit in silence, looking at the wet tablecloth and overturned glasses. The perfect table setting is in shambles, just like my life.

CHAPTER TWENTY-FIVE

I'm not sure how I made it home. I drove through the side streets, knowing the tears would obstruct my vision and the sobbing would slow down my reaction time. This is not a night to battle the freeways.

Parked safely in front of my house, I let my head fall on the steering wheel as I replay the meeting over and over.

He was thrilled to see me. I showed him the pictures, and he almost grinned. That wasn't the response I'd expected. It wasn't until I began yelling at him about integrity and infidelity that he finally responded.

I expected him to be angry about his lack of privacy. I expected him to rant about trust, but I didn't expect him to tell me I was wrong and storm out. He never defended himself. He went as far as saying he was going to keep the girl in his life.

The saddest thing was how I had to tell him I might be carrying his child. His only response was that he had rights. I wish things could've been different.

The envelope he threw on the table has a red stamp on it that says, "Confidential." I tossed it in my bag before I fled the restaurant.

I'm sure the staff wondered where we went as both of us bolted from the dining room.

I LIFT my head to see a shadow cross the street. The silhouette of a man is outlined against the porch light of my neighbor. He stops and stares at me for a few minutes before he turns and disappears. A chill runs down my spine. With my bag in my hand and my keys laced through my fingers, I'm ready if someone attacks. I exit the car and quickly make my way into the house.

The envelope slips from my bag as I toss everything onto the couch. I wanted to rip it open at the table. What could be so important that, in the middle of everything, he needed to give me this? I look at the red stamp on the front, and my head spins. This is what he was doing. He wasn't cheating on me. He was trying to help me. I know what I'll find before I even open the envelope. I slip my finger under the flap and tear the closure free.

My hands are visibly shaking as I pull the thick packet out of the envelope. The front page is blank except for the words,

Taylor Collins
Private Investigator
Case # 1531
Emma Lloyd

I turn the page and read the story of my life.

Interview with Holly Maxwell – Friend of Adrianne Helms

Ms. Maxwell recalled Adrianne with clarity. They were best friends until the day Ms. Helms left for parts unknown. She indicated Ms. Helms had a long-term relationship with a boy named Tate Smith. School records show that Tate Smith attended Rockville High School at the same time as Adrianne Helms. Adrianne dropped out of school halfway through her senior year.

According to Ms. Maxwell, rumor had it, Adrianne was carrying Tate Smith's child. She said the two had planned to run away together. When asked about Tate Smith's whereabouts, Ms. Maxwell stated he was sent to a military academy to finish off his senior year of high school. Ms. Maxwell offered that it didn't surprise her Tate disappeared. His family wouldn't have been happy about an unexpected pregnancy. She was shocked Adrianne ended up marrying a stranger. No one had heard of Daniel Lloyd before what she describes as "the incident."

The Incident – Adrianne Helms and Daniel Lloyd

After an extensive investigation into Adrianne and Daniel's marriage, it is clear that the two had no prior relationship. There is no record of Daniel Lloyd living in or near Dallas at the time of his marriage to Ms. Helms. Most interesting is that there is no record of a Daniel Lloyd with the social security number given on the marriage license. I did an exhaustive search, and it seems as if Mr. Lloyd appeared out of thin air.

The ding of an incoming text draws me away from the report.

What's happening? Anthony sent out an SOS to Damon. He left a few minutes ago. Kat

I can't explain right now. I made a huge mistake, and I think I may have lost him forever. I'm glad Damon is going to him. Oh, Kat, I screwed up.

I'm on my way.

No other texts are exchanged. I pick up the report and keep reading.

Interviews with neighbors of Adrianne Helms—Sam Watson, Lorene Helberg

Interviews were conducted with two neighbors who lived in the neighborhood at the time. Both stories are the same. Adrianne was caught in bed with Daniel. Her screams alerted her family. The father walked in to see his daughter naked beneath the man. Once they caught them in a compromising situation, she was married off to Daniel in what can only be described as a shotgun wedding.

Oh, my God... my mom was raped and married off to a stranger. Who in the hell was Daniel Lloyd?

An investigation into Tate Smith?

Tate Smith—son of Congressman Teague Smith of the 12th District and his wife, Heidi

The investigation shows Tate being transferred in the middle of his senior year to Melbin Military Academy in Boston, Massachusetts. There is no reason for the transfer listed. Tate was a good student academically but tried to leave the facility several times without permission. Melbin is a strict lockdown facility for rebellious youth. He disappeared on graduation day.

Congressman Smith passed away two years after his son's graduation. I tracked down the mother. She currently lives in Phoenix, Arizona. I visited with her, and she broke her silence after twenty-five years. She indicated Tate had told them he was going to be a father. Teague was furious. He sent Tate to boarding school and hired an ex-convict on parole to compromise the Helms girl. In exchange for the deed, he would receive a new identity, a pretty wife, and a large sum of money to disappear. The Helms' devout faith would allow for nothing less than a wedding. She doesn't know what happened after the incident as the Helms girl was married off and disappeared.

The widow Smith indicated she has only seen her son one time since he left for the Military Academy. He was present at the reading of his father's will, and he immediately donated the money he inherited to a local home for unwed mothers. She has never seen him again. Ironically, they live in the same town.

I located Tate Smith living in Phoenix, Arizona. He is a prominent businessman working in Cyber Security and is married and has a daughter. See the enclosed pictures.

I look through the papers and pull out the pictures at the very back. One is a handsome-looking man with auburn hair. His green eyes almost glow against his fair creamy complexion. The next image is of her, the girl in the photos. She looks like me, only younger. Her hair is a lighter red, but she has her father's eyes—my father's eyes. The information is almost overwhelming. I bury my head in my hands and sob. The front door opens, and Kat runs in.

"What is it?" she asks as she looks at the papers all around me.

I can't say a word. I pick up the pages of the report I've read and hand them to her. She sits next to me and begins to read. We sit in silence as she reads the beginning of my story and I finish the end.

Meeting with Tate, Amy, and Layla Smith

I met with the Smith family at a local restaurant. After explaining my purpose, Mr. Smith broke down and cried. He indicated that he'd searched nonstop for four years, looking for Adrianne and their child. He married his wife, and they both continued their search for years. The new identity made it impossible for them to find Adrianne and the child. Daniel Lloyd technically doesn't exist. Layla is the child of Amy and Tate Smith, and she is twenty years old. As requested, I have asked the family not to contact Emma until you talk to her. They have agreed not to make physical contact. They are looking forward to uniting their family.

Uniting their family. These people are my family. I have a sister and a father who wanted me and loved me. He searched for us. I was a love child. I think about how my mom loved to look into my eyes, and now I know why. It was because when she saw me—she saw him.

I look over at Kat and watch as she wipes a tear from her face. She looks up at me and cries. What a pair we are.

"Kat, I accused him of having an affair with my sister. I didn't know she was my sister. I told him he had no integrity. I lost him because I'm young and stupid, and I always expect the worst from people. I didn't give him a chance, and I didn't give him all of me. I held back just enough so that if he hurt me like I expected him to, I wouldn't be completely shattered. In the end, I ruined myself."

Her arms fold around me, and we both cry ourselves to exhaustion.

"Don't give up, Em. Fight for him. Show him he's worth it. Prove to him only you can fill his life, his heart, and his bed."

I pull out my phone and send Anthony a text.

I'm so sorry. I made the biggest mistake of my life. Please forgive me.

I wait for his reply, but nothing comes. I text the address for my doctor's appointment and then send it.

Kat stays the night with me. I think she felt she needed to remain on suicide watch, but I couldn't kill myself because I'm already dead. I died the minute he walked out of the restaurant and told me to leave him alone.

We'd climbed into my bed like we did when we were kids. My mind filled with the investigator's findings. The rest of the report was just a summary. Daniel Lloyd disappeared after my mom's death but left enough money in a trust to pay for the household expenses. When the house sold, he shuffled the money so many places, it was impossible to track. Daniel Lloyd vanished off the face of the earth. He probably emerged as his true identity and went his own way. The only contact anyone has had with him was a note I received years ago. My mind reels from all the information. I wonder who his sister was? Was she his sister? I'll never know.

I WAKE to the warmth of a body spooning mine. I almost believe it's him until I roll over and see the long blonde hair spread across the pillow. Kat had stayed with me all night.

I crawl out of bed quietly. I have so much to do. I went to bed defeated but woke up ready to battle. Daniel Lloyd took everything from my mom because he wanted a new beginning. I'm not letting him take everything from me. My life has been molded out of fear, and I refuse to cower anymore. I messed up, and if I can win Anthony back, I will. He is worth the fight.

I think about Roxy and her family, how parents can ruin so many futures because they thought they knew best. Only your heart can decide whom to love. It's too late for Anthony and Roseanne, but it's not too late for Roxy, and if I can make it happen, I will.

The next several hours are spent calling every police station in Los Angeles County. I finally locate a detective named Bobby Anderson. To my relief, he is the one and only Bobby from Roxy's past. He's still single, and if he can find someone to cover his shift, he will come to prom to catch up with Roxy. He all but admitted he had a secret crush on her throughout high school, but she was out of his league.

I have no intention of telling her. I think prom should have a few surprises.

I wake Kat's lazy butt up and tell her to get ready—we are having a spa day. If I am going to win my man back, it will not be with raggedy nails, frizzy hair, and sallow skin. I'm in desperate need of help.

The only appointment I could get us is at noon, so I hurry and change. I pull my hair back into a messy bun, throw on a pair of jeans, a T-shirt, and sandals. I toss some clothes at Kat and tell her to put a fire under her ass. The day is wasting, and I have to prepare for the fight of my life.

I have one thing left to do before we head out. I sent the original prom invitation to Anthony, but I feel like I need to send him something more personal. I take out a beautiful black note card made of fine linen paper. I scrounge through my junk drawer and find the silver, acid-free marker and write.

Anthony,
You are cordially invited to join Emma at the event of the year. Formal attire is preferred, but I will take you dressed in anything.
Please understand that I'm young and learning.
Remember that you loved me once.
Only you matter to my heart.

My life will be empty without you.

I'm sorry—I would like to trade in my brownie points—can I have another chance?

Your Emma

I place the invitation in the envelope and put it in my purse. I will hand deliver it tomorrow.

Kat and I spend the next three hours getting everything done possible. We've been scrubbed and polished, painted, and patted until our skin glowed and our nails shimmered. I drop Kat off at the house. She jumps directly in her car and heads home to Damon. I race inside to plan my next move.

I read through the packet again and notice my family has left contact information. I sit in front of the computer and send an introductory message to Tate Smith.

Mr. Smith,

This is Emma. My mother was Adrianne Helms. I received the report from Anthony, and I wanted to reach out to you and say hello. I hope I have the opportunity to meet you and your daughter someday. I'd love to hear more about your family and the life you share. Please feel free to contact me.

Emma

I send it and move on to my next task. I need to pick out an outfit for tomorrow. I want to knock Anthony's socks off. I have a doctor's appointment in the morning, but I plan to stalk Anthony at some point, and I want to look nice.

I rummage through my closet and find a sexy outfit that will be suitable for work and capable of making Anthony speechless. I settle on a black pencil skirt with a back slit. The emerald-green scoop neck T-shirt I chose will show off my cleavage without showing too much. It will show just enough to remind him of what the girls look and feel like. I pair the outfit with a cropped jacket that will show off my waist. A pair of tall black pumps will complete the ensemble. I choose several gold chains in varying lengths and a simple pair of gold hoops as accessories.

My next task is to compile a playlist that represents our time together. I'll send him songs daily, reminding him of who we are and who we were. I download the song for today. I send it as a gift, having it delivered directly to him. The first song is Taylor Swift—"Back to December." I've started the playlist off with an apology. I press send and hope he responds.

I get a text immediately, and my heart swells with hope.

What time is your appointment?

It's not what I'd hoped for, but at least he texted.

My appointment is tomorrow at eight in the morning. Are you going to come?

I wait for his response and receive none. The hope I felt has plummeted to a new low. I brush my teeth and get ready for an early night. I spend the rest of the evening picking out flowers to have delivered to him every day this week. It's how he wooed me, and I hope to turn the tables on him. I know he still loves me; I need to break through his angry shell to get to his heart again.

CHAPTER TWENTY-SIX

I wake early and take extra care in getting ready. I moisturize my legs and arms, so they look and feel silky soft. After taming my loose curls, I leave them hanging down my back. I apply my makeup, lining my eyes in the cappuccino-brown pencil that makes my green eyes stand out. The last thing I apply is deep-red lipstick and a coat of sheer gloss. I check myself from all angles in the full-length mirror. Happy with my reflection, I pick up my black handbag and head out. If I leave now, I'll miss the heaviest traffic and will probably arrive a few minutes early.

THE TIME I thought I was going to save by leaving early, I lost when I tried to find a parking place. I end up running down the street in four-inch heels. Rushing through the revolving doors, I come to a dead stop in the lobby. Standing against the marble wall is Anthony with no expression on his face. He leans against the wall with one foot bent and pressed against it. His arms are crossed defensively in front of his chest. He almost looks bored.

"I'm sorry to keep you. I had the toughest time parking and had to run all the way here. I hope you weren't here long." I try to catch my breath as I wait for his reply.

He walks to the elevator and waits for the car to come. When the door opens, we both step in. "What floor?" he asks curtly. He isn't in the mood for small talk.

"Third floor. It's room 302." I watch him push the button to the third floor. The elevator lurches up, making me lose my balance. I nearly topple over in my high heels. He grabs my arm and helps me gain my balance but let's go immediately.

"You should choose more appropriate shoes," he spits out in a vicious voice.

Before I can respond, the car comes to a stop on the third floor. The door opens, and he steps out in front of me and makes his way to room 302. He'd usually walk beside me or lead me, but I guess his anger has influenced his manners.

He steps into the waiting room and stands to the side as I check in with the receptionist. I take a seat in one chair against the wall. He sits as far away from me as possible. I lower my eyes to avoid the tears that threaten to spill. I know I hurt him. I can see it in his eyes. I slowly lift my head to peek in his direction and find him staring at me. My heart skips a beat. As soon as he sees me look at him, he focuses his eyes somewhere else.

A door opens, and a nurse calls my name. I get up quickly and turn to Anthony, asking him if he wants to come in. He looks at me with a level of surprise I didn't expect. *Did he think I'd leave him in the waiting room?* We are directed to a conference room. I take one of the two seats in front of the desk. I pat the handle on the chair next to me. He looks at the chair and then at me before he sits in the empty seat.

Just then, my physician walks in. Carrying several pieces of paper in her hand, she sits at her desk and looks at both of us.

"Good morning, Emma." She holds out her hand and offers it to Anthony. "I'm Dr. Clark."

"I'm Anthony," is all he offers.

"Okay, I assume you are both here for the results of the blood test. The lab faxed them over this morning. Your iron levels are deficient. You are borderline anemic. I am going to prescribe an iron supplement. The news that you're waiting for can be perceived as good or bad. I have no idea where you both sit in your relationship or your desire to have children." She looks to both of us before she continues.

The only thing I hear is the rush of blood in my head and the words of my self-conscience telling me, *Holy shit, you're pregnant.*

She looks down at the lab results to double-check the findings, I assume. "The test is negative, Emma. You're not pregnant," she says.

The news is almost sad. My first reaction is to cry. I swallow the knot in my throat. "Can low iron explain nausea and missed cycles?"

I look at Anthony and see his face is devoid of emotion. I don't know if he's relieved or disappointed. He stands up and leaves without saying a word.

"I take it by his reaction, this is bad news? He looks disappointed." She looks at the papers littering her desk. "Let's get you on an iron supplement and check your levels in a few weeks."

"He's not disappointed. He's probably relieved. We had a nasty breakup on Saturday. I need to discuss birth control options, Dr. Clark. Clearly, the minipill is not working effectively for me. I have no idea when I'll be sexually active again, but I don't want to have another scare. I need to either stop my periods for months or get a regimen in which they come like clockwork. What do you recommend?"

We talk about several options, and after weighing the pros and cons, I decide on the shot. She has the nurse prep the exam room. She leads me into the room and administers the injection.

"Use a second form of birth control for the next week. After that, you should be good to go. Your cycle will be irregular for the first few months but will be less frequent with consistent use. Routine shots will protect you from unwanted pregnancy. In the event you decide you want to get pregnant, you just opt out of your next injection and continue to practice." She gives me a warm smile. "Do you have questions?"

"No, thank you very much." I'm escorted to the front desk, where I pay my bill and make the appointment for my next injection.

I walk out of the office feeling incredibly sad even though the news should've made me happy. I'm not carrying a child out of wedlock and won't have to raise a child on my own. I lean against the wall and take a deep breath. I feel empty and bereft. I've lost Anthony, and now I don't have a part of him to hold on to.

I pull back my shoulders and walk to the elevator. In the end, it's a good thing. I'm just being sentimental and selfish. Having his child would've kept him in my life, in some form, even if it was only visitation and parent-teacher conferences.

I push the button to call the elevator. As I wait for the car to arrive, I hear my inner voice chant, *Fight for him.*

I send the next song on my playlist. "I Knew I Loved You" by Savage Garden travels across invisible wavelengths to his phone. I send him a text message.

Thank you for coming today. I love you.

I don't expect him to reply, and I'm shocked when he does.

What would you have done if you'd been pregnant?

I'd already decided I'd have tried to be a wonderful mother.

If it's any consolation, I think you would've made a wonderful own.

His text leaves me speechless.

The elevator opens to the first floor. In my wildest dreams, I'd have loved to see him standing against the wall—waiting for me. When I enter the lobby, I'm alone.

I stroll to my car, enter the driver's seat, and head into work. The first thing I notice in the garage is that his car is parked in his designated spot right next to Damon's. That means Kat is probably here as well.

I enter the side door and take the most direct path to my small office in the corner, where I turn on the lights, toss my purse in my desk drawer, and dig into the day's work. I am grateful for my small space out of the way.

I hear the heels on the tile floor long before she materializes in my doorway. Kat stands against the doorjamb and smiles at me.

"Well, am I going to be an aunt?" She sees the tears pool in my eyes and comes running to fold me into her arms.

"No, I'm iron deficient, and my hormones are a mess, but I started the shot today, so things should get more regulated soon."

"That's good news, right?" She looks curiously at me.

"You'd think so, but I'm kind of sad. I had time to imagine a beautiful baby boy with brown curls and blue eyes, and I was in love with the idea of him." I tilt my head and shrug my shoulders. "He came to the appointment today, but as soon as the doctor said I wasn't pregnant, he got up and left."

"Give him some time, Em. He's still hurt. He was trying to do something good, and it backfired on him. He'll come around."

"I screwed up, Kat. He's the one, and I may have ruined everything."

"Well, shore up your tears, girl. We've been called into a meeting with Damon and Anthony. Trevor and a representative from the police department will be present as well. Show them all what a powerful woman you are." She gives me a gentle squeeze and then releases me.

"Go ahead of me. I need to touch up my lipstick and make sure I'm presentable."

CHAPTER TWENTY-SEVEN

Kat walks out of my office and leaves me to my own devices. I reach for my purse and take out my compact mirror, pinch my cheeks to give my skin a little color, and reapply my lipstick and gloss. I drag my fingers through my hair and walk toward the conference room.

When I enter the room, I take a quick look around. I see Anthony, Damon, Kat, Trevor, a police officer, and Tom Wakefield. His presence boils my blood. He rises as soon as I enter. He pulls out the chair next to him, but I ignore his gesture and sit at the opposite side of the table.

I sit several chairs down from Anthony. I find my eyes traveling to him, and each time he catches me looking, his eyes dart in a different direction. A weaker girl might have looked at the enormity of the situation and thrown in the towel. I was that girl a few weeks ago, but she got a slap upside the head that straightened her out. I'm not giving up until I've tried everything.

The police officer explains the details of the underage drinking allegations. The reporter takes notes furiously. I don't know who invited him, but in the end, it will be good for Ahz to have him here. On the other hand, I want to slap him upside the head every time he asks a question. He's the reason I'm in the situation I am. *No, you're the reason you're in the situation you're in. You didn't have enough faith in the man you said you loved.* My inner voice is loud and clear today. She's not letting me off the hook, and rightly so. I created this situation, and I need to fix it.

"Emma, do you have any questions?"

I hear my name from somewhere far off. In my thoughts, I've traveled to a quiet place and tuned the entire room out.

"Emma, Damon asked if you had questions." Kat taps my arm, bringing me back to the present.

I glance around the table and find everyone staring at me. "No, I have nothing to ask and nothing to add."

Everyone from the meeting rises and leaves. The only people left are Tom Wakefield, Anthony, and me. They both look at me, and I feel like I'm intruding. I walk to the door to exit. Before I turn the corner, I look over my shoulder and lock eyes with Anthony. He stares at me for a minute and then looks back at Tom.

I listen to the clickety-clack of my heels on the tile floor as I head to my office. Since he will be busy with the reporter for a few minutes, it's the perfect time to sneak into his office and drop off my invite.

The envelope weighs heavily in my hand as I put it in the center of his desk. I see my flowers have arrived. I wonder if he has seen them yet. I can only do what I can do. I have to hope fate will dish out something better than the shit she's given me recently.

I almost make it back to my office when I hear my name called. I turn to see Tom Wakefield advancing toward me.

"Emma, I owe you an apology. I sent you those pictures without actually doing any investigation. I just saw a beautiful woman obviously in love with a rich playboy. I didn't give Mr. Haywood the benefit of the doubt."

"The sin doesn't fall completely on your shoulders, Mr. Wakefield. I didn't give him the benefit of the doubt either. I allowed you to plant a seed of doubt in my mind, and I let it grow into a vine that choked the life out of our relationship."

"I'm sorry. Is there anything I can do?"

"No, I can manage to screw things up enough on my own. I only ask that you do a good job clearing up any doubt about Ahz and the underage drinking allegations."

"I will do that. I'd like to give you a friendly hug, if I may?" He gives me a half smile.

Oh, what the hell? Half of my problem has been that I've held grudges. I reach forward and hug the reporter, who in one moment changed my world. I could hate him, but he taught me a valuable lesson about love, trust, and letting go. I wrap my arms loosely around his shoulders and squeeze gently.

"Have a good day, Mr. Wakefield."

The rest of the day goes by smoothly. I haven't heard from Anthony at all since the appointment. I assume he's left for his corporate office. He trots between the two regularly. I think he was spending more time here lately so he could see me. I believe that will end now that he seems to want to avoid me at all costs.

I gather my things and take my time getting to the garage. Feeling a tap on my shoulders, I turn to find Trevor.

"Chris and I are heading to Trax tonight. It's Monday night, Martini Madness. Do you want to come with us? You look like you could use a drink."

"Does it show that much?" I exhale forcefully through pursed lips. "I really could use a few drinks. Yes, I think I will. What time?"

"We'll meet you there at seven. Roxy is bartending, so she can hook you up with a few good, strong martinis. Take a taxi. I don't want you driving." Trevor escorts me to my car and kisses both of my cheeks.

Trax sounds like a good idea. It will be a better night than the one I had planned. Dancing and getting numbingly drunk sounds so much better than takeout and flannel pajamas.

I spend the drive home listening to music. So many songs remind me of Anthony. I think about tomorrow's playlist selection. I decide on "Just Give Me a Reason" by Pink and Nate Ruess.

Once home, I putter around the house, cleaning everything in sight. It's my therapy. At six o'clock, I call ahead for a cab and change into jeans, ballet flats, and a Journey T-shirt. I'm dressed to get shit-faced drunk.

The taxi honks as soon as it arrives. With the house locked up, I rush down the sidewalk thinking about a numbing night of music that's way too loud and drinks that are way too strong.

Roxy seems to run from end to end of the bar. Monday nights are hopping at Trax. She sees me and nods her head, then points to the end of the bar, where I slide into the one empty seat.

"Good to see you. What can I get you?" She wipes the counter in front of me and lays down a cocktail napkin.

"Lemon drop martini and keep them coming. I'm not driving, and if I pass out, I'll depend on you to get me home."

"Fair enough. Stay close to me, or you might be some girl's new dream come true." She winks at me.

"Hell, given my track record with men lately, I might switch sides. I couldn't have any worse luck."

"Don't borrow trouble. Here come Chris and Trevor. They can babysit you for a while." She sets my glass in front of me and dashes off to fill another order. I can see how she stays so thin. She must run a marathon each night she works.

"Look at who's come to the other side. Welcome home, sis." Chris leans in for a smooch.

I spend the next few hours tossing back one martini after another. I dance with anyone who will dance with me. I don't care if they are male, female, gay, or straight. I need to have some fun. Mostly, I end up dancing in between Chris and Trevor, who make me the center of their gay boy sandwich. They cage me between their arms and dance around me.

Sitting at the bar, on a brief respite from dancing, I watch as they hold each other in their arms. Chris's head pressed on Trevor's shoulder. It's an incredibly intimate moment, and I almost feel guilty watching it. Chris raises his head and looks into Trevor's eyes. Their lips meet in a kiss. *Holy shit*—I had no idea watching two men in love kiss could be so hot. My heart clenches. I want to be kissed like that.

In my drunken state, I send a text to Anthony.

I'm watching two men practically make love on the dance floor, which reminded me of you.

I pressed send.

What? How would two gay men remind you of me? Where are you?

I want you to kiss me.

Where are you?

Thank God for autocorrect. Who knows what I'm actually texting, but I hope it makes sense. I order another drink from Roxy. She gives me a concerned look, but when I tell her to make it, she does. She knows I'm in pain.

I see the light on my phone illuminate in the dim club. I see his name and answer. "Heyyyyy, you called. I'm trying to drink you away. I'm doing my best to get you back, but you're lost."

"Emma, where are you?"

"I'm at trash with Tigger and Cribs," I say, but the words seem to fall out of my mouth in a jumble.

"Put someone else on the phone, now!"

I tap the man sitting next to me. "Heyyyy, my ex-boyfriend wants to talk to you. He's adorable and has a big you-know-what." I hand the phone to him and lay my head on the bar. I can hear things around me, but I can't lift my head to engage. I've hit the place I've been trying to reach all night. I'm comfortably drunk and oblivious.

I hear his sexy voice. It must be my mind playing tricks. I listen the best I can, but nothing makes sense.

"Roxanne, what are you doing here?" It's his voice.

"I work here, stud. What about you? Batting for the other side now?"

"No, I'm coming to take this one home."

"I'll take her. She made me promise to get her home if she couldn't do it herself."

"No need for you to go out of your way. Besides, I don't think she needs to sleep on the bar until closing."

"She's my roommate," I hear her say.

"The irony of that is too much for me to process right now. How much does she owe you?"

"She already paid. She started a tab. If you're taking her home, make sure she has a trash can next to the bed. I imagine she's going to feel pretty awful in the morning."

I feel someone pick me up and cradle me in strong arms. I snuggle into his chest and inhale. I raise my eyes and look into his grim face to see it's him.

"What?" He puts my head against his chest before I can say another word. I hear him talk to a few other people, and then there is cool air and silence.

The next thing I know, my clothes are being pulled off me. First, go my shoes, and then my pants. My shirt is being lifted above my head. I hear a groan and wonder where it came from. My body is moved into the bed, and the sheet is drawn over my near nakedness. The bed dips as he sits next to me. His hand brushes my hair away from my face. I open my eyes to look into his.

"Thank you, Anthony. I'll always love you. There'll be no one else for me." My eyes fill with tears. If this is a dream, I don't want to wake up. I want him here, no matter how I can have him.

"Shh, go to sleep. You probably won't remember much of this tomorrow. I'm pretty sure you're not going to feel well." He pushes my hair behind my ear. "You're such a funny girl. I love you, Emma. I do." I feel the soft touch of lips against my forehead and then nothing.

I WAKE with the worst headache of my life. On my nightstand are a glass of water and two painkillers. Thank God for Roxy. I pop the pills into my mouth and guzzle the water. My initial response is nausea but thank goodness that settles quickly.

I reach for my phone and see Trevor and Chris's messages, both making sure I was okay. *What in the hell did I do last night?* I drank entirely too much.

I grab my head to stop the pounding and climb out of bed then quickly shower and dress in something nice. I can't lose my focus on Anthony. It's bad enough I dreamed of him all night—him telling me he loved me was a glorious dream. If I thought I could conjure him every night, I'd drink myself into a stupor.

Not wanting to be late to work, I make a quick trip through the drive-thru for a breakfast sandwich and a coffee, then head into Ahz.

The first person I run into is Trevor. I hold up my hand as I pass him. "Not a word," I warn. I walk into my office and close the door. My first task is to send him the song for the day, so I send "I Need Your Love" by Ellie Goulding and Calvin Harris before closing my phone and dig into my work for the day.

When my day ends, I head home and straight for bed. I pass Roxy as I enter the hallway. "Thanks for getting me home, Roxy."

"I didn't bring you home. Anthony did. Don't you remember?" She sits up on the couch and tilts her head. Her eyes are as big as saucers. "You don't remember. You texted him, and he came and got you. He brought you home and tucked you in. He didn't leave until I got home. He was worried you'd get sick and drown in your vomit."

I groan inwardly and take the walk of shame to my bedroom. I shed my work clothes and don my flannel pajamas. I pick out tomorrow's song and set up the queue to have it sent automatically. I decide to do that for the rest of the week. I already know what I want him to hear.

Wednesday, he'll hear "Dreaming with a Broken Heart" by John Mayer. I know it's a song about a man, but I believe he felt that way when I blindsided him by my distrust.

Thursday, I'm sending him "Still into You" by Paramore. The message here is that I still love him and want him back.

Friday, he will receive the song "Somewhere Only We Know" by Lily Allen. It's almost like me begging him to go back to the place we were before we got here. Saturday will be the last song I send. I choose "Just Say Yes" by Snow Patrol. I hope it's self-explanatory. I want him to say yes to the prom, but mostly to me.

It's hard not knowing what someone might be thinking. I wish I knew what was on his mind.

CHAPTER TWENTY-EIGHT

Wednesday gives my heart a little leap of hope as I wake up to a text from Anthony.

I'm just checking in to see that you are feeling better.

If you are referring to my drunken madness from Monday night, then yes, I've finally recovered. Thank you for taking care of me. It warms my heart to know that you cared enough to come to my rescue. I only wish I'd been sober enough to have noticed. I miss you, and I love you. I'm sorry.

There has never been a question in my mind about my love and concern for you. It was that same love and concern that got me in trouble.

I was such a stupid girl.

Don't beat yourself up; we all have our moments. Have a good day, Emma.

You too, Anthony.

The rest of the day has me smiling like a loon and dancing on air.

It was just a cordial text, but it was more than I'd heard from him since our fight.

The next few days pass in a blur. I haven't seen or heard from Anthony, and that makes my heart twist. I received an email from Tate and Layla. They were genuinely nice and gave me lots of information about their lives. We are planning a trip to get together soon. I keep forgetting to ask him if he was the one standing in front of my house. I'll have to assume he was visiting since the stranger has not been back since I contacted them.

It's Saturday morning, and I have no idea if I'll have a date for the dance tonight. I haven't heard a word from Anthony since Wednesday. I've tried to jump in with both feet. I've done what I can without being completely in his face. There is a fine line between letting him know I'm all in and kidnapping him to lock him in his house until he says he loves me. Maybe I should've gone with the kidnapping plan after all.

I let Roxy sleep in until two o'clock before I decide to wake her butt up. She has a prom to go to, and she doesn't know Bobby Anderson will be there. I'm so excited he will come. He called my office yesterday and confirmed. He also asked me what color dress Roxy was wearing because he wanted to buy her a wrist corsage. I recommended white since that would go with everything.

"What are you wearing tonight?" I sit on the edge of her bed and bounce, forcing her to wake up.

"Do I have to go?" she groans. "I thought it would be fun, but now I'm not sure. I don't even have a date."

"I don't have a date either. Roxy, will you go to prom with me?" I ask sweetly.

"I have nothing to wear." She rolls over onto her stomach. I swat her ass hard, and she shrieks. "I thought about just wearing one of my regular dresses."

"You can't wear a sundress to prom. Get up. Between the two of us, we can come up with something. I'm bigger than you, but I like dresses cut on the bias, which means they hang well on most figures. You only need to get close in size. The cut of the dress does the rest." I pull the covers back and look at her figure. She's wearing yoga pants and a tank top, so it's easy to see the shape of her body. "What color do you want to wear? I've got them all."

"I'm partial to blue and silver," she says as she stretches and yawns.

My lips turn into a wicked grin. I have the perfect dress for her.

"Emma, this dress is obscene. Are you sure the tape will hold my boobs in?" She looks at herself in my sinful blue dress. It's the dress Anthony said was criminal and unfair to the male population of the world. Standing next to her, I feel like the duckling next to the swan. She looks beautiful.

"This dress looks amazing on you." I add a little silver sparkle to her eyeshadow and call her done for the night. Focusing on Roxy has given me something to do. I've been able to spend my entire afternoon without once thinking about Anthony and whether he'd come tonight. I'm resigned to the fact that he probably won't show up. I hurt him, and after what he went through with Roseanne, he's probably once bitten, twice shy. I just hope we can eventually be friends. I want him to be with me, but if the only way I can have him is as a friend, then I will have to settle for that.

"Do you want me to drive?" Roxy asks as she peeks her head into my room.

"No, I ordered a car. We can't drive ourselves to prom. What kind of date would I be if I didn't take care of my girl?" I pull my hot-pink dress off the hanger, slipping it up and over my hips. It's a ridiculous dress. It's short and slinky, showing off lots of leg, and covers very little. It was hot in its day. I'm representing Generation Y. "Can you zip me up?" I turn my back to her, and she glides the zipper closed. I'm surprised it still fits. I slip on my strappy silver sandals and turn to look at myself in the mirror.

I'm not at the top of my game right now, but I'll do in a pinch. I leave my hair in loose curls that fall down my back and touch up my makeup. I spray on an ample amount of perfume and declare that I'm ready.

THE LIMOUSINE DROPS us off at the front. The doorman greets us, checks our ID cards, and stands aside for us to enter. We take the elevator to the third floor. The club is beautiful; it's exactly the way I imagined it would be.

They greet us at the entrance with sashes and tiaras. I want every woman who enters to be the prom queen and every man to be the king. All guests will receive a sash and a crown. It's my prom, and I want everyone to feel special.

The music is already booming. We arrived early so I can make sure everything is in order. I look around and soak in the atmosphere. It took a bit of work, but I represented every class from our guest list. Hanging from the ceiling are signs saying, "Class of…" and various years are highlighted from 1970 to the present. There is a photographer set up to take portraits in the right corner because you can't have the prom without pictures.

A fabulous champagne fountain sits in the far-left corner, and a table full of my favorite Anthony Haywood appetizers is next to it. It's an open bar tonight, and I have hired taxis to accommodate those who drink too much. After the drunk driving accident of late, I'm taking no chances.

Roxy follows me around. She looks darling in her tiara and sash. "Welcome to Ahz." I hold my hands out, showcasing it before guiding her to the champagne fountain to get us both a drink. "Here's to new beginnings." I raise my glass in a toast.

"This is fabulous, Emma." Her eyes look around the entire room and settle on the bar.

"It's a great bar. Do you want to check it out?" I know she wants to see how it's set up and how the bartenders run it, so I guide her over to introduce her to the two men serving tonight. "Roxy, this is Chaz and Terrance. Guys, this is Roxy. She bartends at Trax." With introductions made and tours complete, we stroll around the club and find ourselves back at the bar. We take up space like wallflowers, leaning against the granite top. Our eyes lock on the door. I'm watching for several people, but I have no idea who Roxy is waiting for.

"Are Trevor and Chris coming?" She sips her champagne and returns her gaze to the door.

"Yes, Kat and Damon will be here as well. You won't be stuck with just me tonight." I pat her arm as if trying to comfort her. I secretly smile to myself because I know who is coming for her, and I'm excited to see her face.

I look around and watch as people pour into the club. This is by invitation only. Who wouldn't want to come? I spend my time checking out all the dresses and tuxedos. It's so funny what some people will wear. Out of the corner of my eye, I see Chris and Trevor enter. They are in matching tuxedos. I was convinced one of them would wear a dress. Chris is in white tails, while Trevor is in black. They look adorable. They see me and Roxy standing by the bar and travel a straight line toward us.

"Holy smokes, Roxy, are those going to spill out if you bend over?" Trevor asks as he looks at her cleavage.

"Emma guarantees me the girls are secure. I'll trust her until proven otherwise."

They order a drink and chat. I look around and see the doorman trying to get my attention.

"I'll be right back." I leave them to their chitchat and walk to the door to see why I'm needed. I'm hoping Bobby has arrived.

The doorman brings me to the hallway, where a very tall man stands. I go over to him and ask, "Are you, Bobby?" A big grin spreads across his face.

"How did you know?" I look down at the white wrist corsage in his hand and smile. "Ah yes, the giveaway. Is Roxanne here?"

"Yes, she is in the club, standing by the bar with my brother and his boyfriend." His eyes lift in surprise. "We are an open love family, Bobby. I hope you don't have an issue with that."

"No, not at all. I just wouldn't have expected a Somerville to be open to mixing."

"Didn't you hear? Roxy is the black sheep of the Somervilles. Let's go get your date." We walk through the door where Bobby is given a crown and a prom king sash, and then I lead him to Roxy.

Her back is turned to us when we arrive. I place Bobby behind her as I step to her side. "Hey, girl, this really hot single guy just came in looking for a date. Since I will probably be busy tonight and won't be able to spend much time with you, I thought maybe I'd introduce the two of you."

"No way. You got me here, but I'm not hooking up with some strange dude to ease your guilty conscience. I'll hang with my boys." She watches as Chris and Trevor look above her head. "He's standing behind me, isn't he?" she asks as she rolls her eyes.

I watch as her skin flushes red from her navel to her forehead. She slowly turns around. Her eyes travel past me as she rotates 180 degrees and stares at his broad chest. I watch as recognition crosses her face.

"Nice to see you, Roxanne. How long has it been—five years—more?" He opens the clear plastic box and removes the corsage. Taking her hand in his, he gently places the flowers over her wrist and kisses her knuckles. I watch as her knees almost buckle.

"You guys have fun," I say, leaving them at the bar staring into each other's eyes. *How cute are they?*

I stroll around the club. It seems like everyone is enjoying themselves. *Everyone but me.* It would appear that I'm the only person going stag to prom tonight. I find myself at the bar listening to the music and watching people dance. The DJ has kept the music lively. I'm going to have to ask him to throw in a few slow songs for the lovers in the group.

The idea of lovers makes me think of Anthony. I miss making love to him. It's been weeks since I touched him. If he isn't here yet, he probably isn't coming. I look to the door one last time. What I see shocks me. My feet move on their own accord.

"Oh, my God. Are you truly here?" I stare at the handsome man standing in front of me. His eyes are full of happiness, and my heart is ready to explode.

"Emma, is that you?" He grabs me and pulls me into his arms.

"Dad, I think you're killing her," the beautiful redheaded woman says. The man embracing me lets go. He holds me at a distance and looks at me long and hard.

"Emma, I'm Tate. I'm your father. This is your sister, Layla. And this is my wife, Amy." I look from person to person and see the joy on all three faces. Tears begin to stream down my cheeks.

CHAPTER TWENTY-NINE

"How did you get here? Who sent the invite?"

Layla bounces like she can't wait to tell me. "Your boyfriend sent us the information and tickets to attend. He's the nicest man and cute, too. You're a lucky girl," she gushes with enthusiasm.

"Yes, I was a lucky girl." Not wanting to sour the happy reunion vibe, I ignore my sadness and embrace the moment. I reach into the box on the entry table and pull out three sashes, two tiaras, and a crown. I accessorize the Smith family and guide them to the photographer. "Let's take a family photo," I suggest. The thought of having a family brings a goofy smile to my face.

We stand under the floral archway and smile for the camera. In front of us, making faces, are Damon, Kat, Chris, and Trevor. I guide my new family to my old family and introduce everyone. Layla seems thrilled to death to have two new gay brothers and a sister who has a wealthy fiancé. We chat for over an hour. They are amazing people. I'm shocked at the generous nature of Amy, who is willing to open her family to a stranger. Layla is hysterical, and I can't wait to get to know her better. Tate is beyond my wildest dreams. I can see why my mom fell in love with him.

He brought several pictures of my mom as a teenager with him, and I'm touched by his thoughtfulness. She was stunning as a young girl. I always thought she was a beautiful woman, but she was my mother, so I thought maybe I was biased.

Tate asks Amy to dance, and I send Chris and Trevor to dance with Layla. I excuse myself so that I can talk to the DJ. I ask him to slow the pace a bit for the couples who might want to share a moment. I look around the crowded room; there are hundreds of couples on the massive dance floor. I scan the space for him and resign myself once again to the fact that he's not coming. In the corner, I see Roxy locked lip to lip with Bobby. I smile at the sweetness of a lost love that has been found.

I slide up to the bar and order a martini. I'm not driving, so I might as well be drinking. The DJ says something over the loudspeaker. I'm not paying much attention, but I hope it's to announce the start of some romantic music. I pick up my martini and toss it back. I hear the DJ say something about playlists. I think about the songs I sent Anthony last week. I'd hoped he could find it in his heart to forgive me. "All of Me" by John Legend plays. I bury my head in my hands and exhale. *I love this song.*

"Can I have this dance?" I hear his voice. I don't want to turn around in fear that I may be conjuring him from my want. Can you do that? Can you want something so badly, your mind makes it materialize?

"Emma—babe, dance with me. Listen to this song and tell me you're ready."

I still don't turn around. My heart swells with extreme emotion. "I can't dance with you. I promised this special man I'd wait for him. He's late, but I know in my heart he'll show up. He's worth the wait. I keep asking myself why he's taking so long."

"He was waiting to see if you were ready to jump in with both feet. He wants to know you're not going to turn around and run when things get tough. He needs to be sure you love him as much as he loves you."

"I do." I slowly turn and see a gorgeous man standing in front of me. His black tuxedo is perfect, and his hot pink cummerbund and bowtie are the exact color of my dress. My eyes take him in from his smile to his hot pink Converse sneakers.

"You're late," I say as a tear runs down my cheek.

He brushes it away. "I had to wait for my Chucks to be delivered. My date was precise in her requests." He smiles at me, and I melt. He pulls me to the dance floor and signals to the DJ to replay the song. I dance in his arms as if we are the only ones in the room. His lips lean down to brush mine. "Did you say I do? I haven't asked, my love."

I stop and look into his eyes. "I don't understand." My confused look sends a smile to his face.

"I went to Phoenix to find your dad, not to cheat on you. Your sister is cute, but she's not you. I wanted to give you your family. I knew in my gut they existed. I asked him for his blessing, even though he'd never met you." His hand palms my cheek. "I told him what an amazing woman you are and how my life will never be whole until you become mine completely. Do you understand what I'm asking you, Emma?"

I look at him with tears spilling from my eyes. "I do."

"You understand, or you *do*?"

"Both." I fall into his warm embrace. We stand in the middle of the dance floor until John Legend completes the perfect love ballad. As the song finishes, he drops to his knee and places a large pink diamond on my finger. It's not a traditional stone, but there is nothing traditional about us.

"Let's say goodbye to everyone." He pulls me toward the edge of the room, where my family and friends wait.

"Where are we going? You just got here." I ask. His arm wraps snuggly around my waist as he leads me through the room. He pulls me off to the side so we can talk in private for a moment.

"I came late to give you time with your family and friends. First, we're going home so I can make love to you. Then we're heading to Vegas. I'm not letting you get away again, babe. I'm taking no chances."

"Why did you make me suffer all week?"

"I wasn't trying to make you suffer, Emma. I just wanted you to have space to think. You once told me if you squeeze a chick too hard, you'll squeeze it to death. I don't want you to feel suffocated by me. I was hoping the time away would help you see how much we need one another. I didn't want my presence to influence your decision."

"I thought you didn't love me anymore."

"How could you think that? I was angry the day we had our fight, but I told you how much I loved you Monday when I brought you home from Trax."

"I don't remember anything. I just hoped you would get my flowers, listen to my songs, and forgive me."

"You were forgiven the minute I saw you running into the doctor's appointment. You do need to wear more practical shoes. By the way, our house smells like a flower shop. I may have to give you a raise to pay your florist bill."

"Why did you run out the door at the doctor?"

"Somewhere inside, I was hoping you were pregnant. I was so disappointed. When you weren't pregnant, I thought maybe I'd lost you forever. I was such an idiot.

"I wanted to surprise you with your family. I should've just told you up front, and none of this would have happened. I'm sorry, Emma."

"I'm sorry, too, Anthony. I've done a lot of growing in the last few weeks. I love you, and I never want to live without you. I'm glad you came to my prom. You're the best date ever."

We say goodbye to everyone. I give my dad, his wife, and my sister a hug and promise to visit Phoenix next week when we return from our trip. Kat hugs me hard and releases me. She informs me my bag is packed and ready to go. Of course, she knew. I look at Chris and Trevor, only to find them both in tears. They are hand-to-hand and hip-to-hip. I can't find Roxy; she's disappeared. Someone else is going to have to notify her I won't be home for a while.

"Let's go, baby. I can't wait any longer." He pulls me from the group and throws me over his shoulder. It's quite a turn-on. This whole caveman routine becomes him. I smile at everyone I pass, knowing this is the beginning of the rest of my life.

I WAKE up in Anthony's arms. My body is sated, and my heart is full. I lift my hand and look at the ring on my finger. It's perfect. He's perfect. I shift my body, so I am looking at him. He pulls me tight against his chest, the smell of him softly wafting through my nose. I am home in his embrace.

He rolls back, pulling me on top of him. I lay my head on his chest. I look at the nightstand by the bed. Our picture from the evening before sits proudly. We are dressed in our prom clothes, with Elvis standing directly behind us. The banner above our heads reads "Just Married."

Nothing Anthony and I do is traditional; from the way we met to the way we married is simply who we are.

He told me we had some papers to sign before we married. I can't blame him for wanting to protect his assets. I'd expected to sign a prenup before we said I do. What surprised me was that when the lawyer met us at the house, it was to sign half of everything he owned over to me. He only smiled and said he was jumping in with both feet. He earned a lifetime of brownie points with that action.

He informed me there was no risk in giving me everything. I'd never have time to leave him because he planned to keep me barefoot, pregnant, and in bed. The kitchen was his and was off-limits to me. How can you say no to that?

Many people would wonder why I rushed to the altar with Anthony. My only answer would be that *he's the one*. My mom didn't get to be with her true love, and I wasn't missing out on the chance to be with mine.

So, we locked ourselves in our room in Las Vegas for an entire week. Although I couldn't get pregnant for several months because of my recent birth control shot, I was willing to practice. They say practice makes perfect. I say perfect practice makes perfect and practice we did.

Next up is *Yours to Protect*

OTHER BOOKS BY KELLY COLLINS

A Pure Decadence Series

Yours to Have

Yours to Conquer

Yours to Protect

A Pure Decadence Collection

Recipes for Love

A Tablespoon of Temptation

A Pinch of Passion

A Dash of Desire

A Cup of Compassion

A Dollop of Delight

A Layer of Love

Recipe for Love Collection 1-3

Recipe for Love Collection 4-6

ABOUT THE AUTHOR

International bestselling author of more than thirty novels, Kelly Collins writes with the intention of keeping love alive. Always a romantic, she blends real-life events with her vivid imagination to create characters and stories that lovers of contemporary romance, new adult, and romantic suspense will return to again and again.

For More Information
www.authorkellycollins.com
kelly@authorkellycollins.com

Printed in Great Britain
by Amazon